# THE EMPEROR'S LESSON

J. K. EVERETT

PUBLISHED BY KJK PUBLISHING

*"While we must, by all available means, prevent the overthrow of the government, we should avoid planting and cultivating too many thorns in the bosom of society."*

— ABRAHAM LINCOLN

# CONTENTS

# PART I

Governor Jason Singleton opened his eyes, struggling to orient himself. The last thing he remembered was walking along the small lake near his home. This was not home. Above him was a set of close-set bars, and above the bars was a dark wooden ceiling. As he raised his head, he could see more bars just past his feet. Above him was some dense plastic-like material draped over the top bars that cascaded down to the bottom of the bars on all four sides. He could see that he was surrounded by a cage but could see nothing beyond the opaque material. He raised up, sat on the edge of an old, musty cot, and suddenly realized he was cold. All he had on was the slacks, sports shirt, and jacket he had been wearing on the walk. It was obviously not enough clothing for this level of cold. He looked around at the sparse decor. Nothing but a bucket on the floor in the corner, the cage, the cot, the cold, and him.

"Hey," he called out. "Is anyone there?" There was no answer. He got up and walked toward the door of the cage. He could see nothing beyond the small space of his enclosure. He tried the door, and when it didn't open, he grabbed the bars with both hands and shook them gently. The bars stood firm. He shook the bars harder, to no avail. Bewildered, as panic overwhelmed him, he reached for his cell phone, but it was not in his pocket. After thoroughly searching himself, he went back to the cot to look for it, but it was not in or under the cot. His eyes swept the dimly lit cage floor. He heard a sound, and he nervously turned to face it.

"If you are looking for your phone, it's gone," an electronically distorted voice said from the other side of the plastic. "Your experts say there is a chance you can get brain cancer from using one of those. So, for your own safety, I disposed of it for you. You're welcome."

"What? Who are you? What am I doing here?" the governor demanded. Grabbing the bars again and shaking them, he yelled, "Do you know who I am? I can tell you that people are looking for me right now. You're not going to get away with this."

The voice calmly said, "Listen to you, Governor, giving orders to me like I work for you. In fact, in your new reality. YOU work for ME. Your childish temper tantrum does not impress me. I am getting my chance to be YOU. In here with me, it is you who is insignificant. I am sure people are looking for you. As to you being found and me being punished, I'm willing to pay the price for being me, just like YOU are going to pay a price for being YOU."

Stepping away from the bars in fright, the governor asked, "What do you mean? Who are you? What do you want?"

"Who I am is not important," the voice said. "If it helps you to have something to call me, you can call me emperor. Do you know that is what we, and many others, call you?"

"What do you mean? Emperor? I'm the governor, God damn it!" the governor said with increasing anger and astonishment.

"You are called 'the emperor' because you do what you want to do to the people under your authority. You and your supporters' control everything. The other half of your subjects, the ones who disagree with you and your edicts, have no say in what happens. You decide while the rest of us must accept your superior wisdom and your mandates, regardless of whether they go against our beliefs or harm us financially. You have pissed off a lot of people—ones who feel they have no representation or voice. To us, WE have been YOUR victims. So, you ask who I am? I am THAT voice, that voice—representing all of us who you do not recognize. But you are going to have to listen now. Your reality now is that I am YOUR Emperor."

With concern in his voice, the governor said, "I don't know what you have in mind, but I WILL be found, and YOU, whoever you are, will be the one locked up in a cage, and for a very long time."

The voice chuckled with amusement. "You know, your Highness, you should just relax. There is nothing to worry about. That is unless you are thinking of all those reasons why you should be concerned about being totally dependent upon someone like me. But then, that is the problem, isn't it? You and your intellectual pygmies think you are the solution to all of mankind's problems. With enough tax money, the power of your office, and your majority in both houses of the legislature, you can do any damn thing you want. You folks even removed the provision for issues to be put on the ballot for the citizens of your state to vote on when they disagree with you. You are further locking your party into power by being able to remove opposition candidates from election ballots."

The voice continued, "What other kinds of countries do things like that? I can tell you WHAT they are NOT; they are not representative democracies! But that's your objective, is it not? To have total control over the lives of the people of this state, to bend them to your will, to force them to accept your worldview. You showed us, didn't you? You can do what you want. WE, the other folks, the 'unwashed' in your eyes, have not been able to do a thing about it. You believe we are not capable of thinking for ourselves or participating in our own governance. As of now, this moment, at least for you, that changes."

The governor started to speak but was cut off by the power of the voice; "And speaking of governance and ballots"—irritation revealed in the rising level of the voice— "you really put one over on the voters of this state when you created the opportunity for the illegal immigrants vote in your elections, didn't you? Yeah, I know, 'illegal immigrant' is an outlawed term, but I digress. I understand that most of the citizens of this state don't know what you've done, but WE DO!"

"What are you talking about?" the governor yelled.

"You know exactly what I'm talking about," the voice continued. "Or maybe you're not sure WHICH sleight of hand I'm talking about."

"Then, clear it up for me, so I can tell you you're wrong," the governor replied smugly.

The voice said, "On the voter registration form, there's a question asking if the person voting is a citizen."

"Yes, that's true," said the governor.

The voice continued, "There's also a notice over on the left side of the registration form that states there's a $5,000 fine for falsifying that box, correct?"

"Yes," said the governor, "anyone falsifying that statement would be subject to that fine. That proves you're wrong when you say we're letting undocumented residents vote."

"That's what you want us all to believe, but it's not true, is it?" challenged the voice. "The state gives driver's licenses to illegal immigrants. Is that a true statement?"

The governor said, "Yes if they have an address representing a residence. We do that because they need a license to get essential services."

"Exactly," the voice added, "and with a driver's license and an address, an illegal immigrant can vote in our elections."

"That's not true," said the governor, "they would be subject to a $5,000 dollar fine. You just said so yourself."

The voice countered, "That is what you tell people, and that's what the legitimate citizens think. They think that if an illegal got caught voting, they would be hit with a big fine, right?"

The governor answered, "Yes because it is true."

The voice said, "But there really isn't much of a risk of getting caught, is there?"

"What do you mean?" said the governor. "I think it's a big deterrent!"

"At least you are sticking with the party line." The voice said. "It may be somewhat of a deterrent, but the reality is that there is no check to determine whether they are lying, is there? You have directed all the state agencies to ignore legal status in the state. In fact, in your state, it is illegal to ask if they are a citizen. Am I correct?" asked the voice.

"Well, that's true, but they're still taking a big risk," said the governor.

"NO, GOVERNOR! THEY ARE NOT," said the voice, "because you declared that it's illegal to ask them to prove their citizenship. No one in an official capacity can even ask if they are a citizen. According to the election rules, it must be a private citizen that challenges their vote based on citizenship. AND whoever DOES challenge their vote is responsible for proving it! You worked around that $5,000 fine so they could vote very nicely and legally. You just bought more votes for your folks at the expense of all your other citizens."

"If they're caught, they could be fined," said the governor with defiance, "so that's still true."

The voice was not deterred. "Yes, you put that in the penalty language on the registration form and then took the teeth out of it in actual practice. Very sneaky, but it does allow you to do what you want, just like always. All those extra votes will help you stay in power. Is that your definition of democracy? Democracy for those who think the way you do! With all those votes, you don't have to listen to any other side."

"THAT'S NOT TRUE!" the governor said with growing frustration. "I DO listen to everyone. Consider the task force I put in place to 'reduce poverty.' Just one of many task forces and committees I've put in place to involve citizens in understanding and developing solutions to our problems."

"I'm very aware of that committee and the results of their deliberations," said the voice. "You packed the group with everyone who would benefit from the 'reforms' they recommended. You did not include anyone who might object to what they came up with or someone who might have other thoughts about the causes OR the solutions.

"But you don't understand how important the things on our agenda are to our state, our county, and the planet. We can't keep debating these things. We need to act, and act now," said the governor.

"Yes, we have heard your speeches," said the voice, "unlike most citizens who are too busy trying to make a living to pay attention to what you're doing. But WE, me, and my supporters, some living on the edge of poverty themselves and then being forced to pay for others through your committees and programs, pay attention to everything you are doing. We also heard you say we are faced with the imminent collapse of the environment, that whites are all racist, and that we must make atonement for the sins of our predecessors. We cannot let things go the way they are. According to you, Governor, everything is wrong, and you, our 'savior,' must make it right. You must save us from ourselves. And above all, you see all the people of this state, whether they agree or not, as responsible for paying for your righteousness."

"See, you don't understand. Let me tell you—" the governor started but was cut off mid-sentence.

The governor heard footsteps walking away and then silence. He walked rapidly back and forth in the cage, fear and anger increasing. With anxiety driving the speed of his pacing, it took only a few seconds to cross the space defined by the bars. With each step, he thought about what he was going to tell the voice. He would make the voice aware of how much power and authority he had. Even the president of the United States knew him by name and was considering him for an appointment in his cabinet after the next election. *Whoever this person is is a fool to have done what they have done to me. I will show them who they are messing with.*

All that happened for the governor for what seemed like the next several hours was him listening to the sounds of silence and the thoughts in his own head. Finally, he heard steps and leaped up from the cot he had been lying on. He charged toward the sound of the approaching footsteps and began to deliver the speech he had formed while waiting for his captor to return. He charged toward the bars on the side of the cage where the footsteps had stopped. "Listen you! I am the governor. I demand..."

"Stop," said the voice.

The governor continued at full intensity, "I will not stop—" The powerful sound of the voice rising over the governor's own words caused the governor to pause.

"STOP! Not one more word from you. Be silent, or you will be silenced. You need to take a second and look around you. Consider your situation and be very cautious about what you do next."

The governor froze and, after a few seconds, removed his hands from the bars and took a step backward into the cage. The only sound was that of footsteps fading into the quiet of his captivity.

Several hours had passed by the time the voice returned. The governor started to speak, but the voice cut him off. "Enough! I will do the talking, and you'll do the listening. Here's how this is going to work. You are MY subject now, and you will do what I tell you. Failure to do so will have consequences for you. You will have some choices and decisions to make to survive here. How that goes is up to you. I don't care about you any more than you care about me. I care if you survive or not. My belief is that the world would be a lot better off if there were fewer people like you in it. For your own sake, I would not take what I am saying to you lightly. I AM the emperor now! NOT you! To start with, you will find a small scrub brush under the mattress on the cot. Your job is to give the floor of your new home a thorough cleaning."

Erupting toward the bars of the cage, the governor yelled, "I'm NOT going to clean your floor for you, you son of a bitch!"

The voice replied calmly, "Be careful, Governor. You don't know my gender; you may have just violated your own law by misgendering me; it's hard to know sometimes, don't you think? Governor, it is no sweat off my brow if you don't clean your new home, but understand this: if you don't do it, you won't be paid, and, therefore, you will have nothing to eat or drink. Again, I don't care about you. You just need to comply. Whatever you decide now affects only you. I'll be doing just fine, just like YOU were when you were emperor. So do it or don't; it's up to you," said the voice. "You have four hours. Failure to comply will have consequences. I'll be back."

* * *

After what seemed to the governor five or six hours, he heard footsteps approaching the cage. "I see you decided not to do what I asked. I told you would not be paid if you didn't do what you were told. You were told there would be consequences."

The governor was cold and irritated. "My folks are going to find me soon, and YOUR ass will be MINE!" said the governor.

"Ok, I understand," said the voice as the sound of footsteps faded away from the cage. "You still think you are in charge."

The governor heard the shuffle of footsteps as they moved away from his cage until, again, there was complete silence. The governor grabbed the bars and yelled into the plastic drapes,

"When am I going to get something to eat? And I need to go to the bathroom!"

There was no answer.

The governor eventually lay down and slept a disquieted sleep. He was awakened when he heard the footsteps return. The voice answered, "I told you that if you did not do what I told you to do, there would be consequences. The first consequence is that you will not get paid. As a result, you will not get anything to eat or drink. You can use the bucket in the corner to go to the bathroom." The voice stopped talking.

The governor sensed it was turning to leave again. "Wait! Wait, please!" said the governor. "Come on, how about some human decency?"

The voice said, "I told you; I am the emperor now. YOU are MY subject! I will see you when I decide I want to see you. Oh, and one more thing. There's a toothbrush, some water, and a small towel being slid through the bars into your new home. Because of your insolence, you can now use the toothbrush instead of the brush you were given before to clean the floor. If you don't do what you're told, there will be more consequences. I assure you, Governor, you will not like them. I am your emperor, and I am losing patience with you. See, Governor, I have learned from you how to punish people who do not agree with me. If you continue to defy me, these small inconveniences that you have been subjected to will end. Just like in your realm, they will be replaced by increasingly severe punishments for failure to comply with my orders."

As the governor began to speak, he realized he was talking to emptiness.

Several hours later, after the floor had been scrubbed, the voice returned and said, "Well done. You did what I told you to do. You are learning." The governor heard what sounded like a small table being pulled over close to the cage. The voice said, "I am going to pay you $150.00 for your work. From that amount, you will pay for your necessities during your stay here. You will be paid $150.00 every week while you're here."

"Aww, come on," said the governor, "this is bullshit. You can NOT keep me here! You can't treat me like this! I'm hungry, and I'm freezing."

The voice said, "Keep on thinking that way, Governor. See how much it helps you get through your time here. I understand your thinking, though. You may have thoughts similar to the ones your citizens had at the beginning of your reign. We never thought our government would treat us the way you did once YOU took YOUR throne. If you think I won't treat you like you treated us, you are going to be very surprised. In fact, it would give me great pleasure to watch you suffer under the burden of my yoke on your neck."

The governor shot back, "I WILL be found soon! You know that, don't you?"

"That's good," said the voice. "Keep thinking someone is going to come along and rescue you. Hope is a satisfying emotion. Hoping our situation would change helped us go about our lives. But hope didn't make a difference. It was decided that action needed to replace hope. Hope did nothing to help us, but who knows, it might help you. Then again, it may not. Now, do you want the money or not?"

"I'm hungry, and I'm cold," the governor said as he moved closer to the sound of where the table landed.

The voice said, "I cannot do anything about the cold. Of course, you will understand that. You decreed that fossil fuels are evil and must be eliminated. I cannot afford solar panels to produce electricity in this location, and most of those windmills you keep talking about exist only in your dreams. Even if they were in place, the distribution system to deliver the energy from them is years in the future. So, there will be no heat for you. We would not want to contribute to the environmental collapse you have so publicly and passionately stated is imminent, would we?" asked the voice.

"There is no source of energy here for you other than some battery-powered lights. Think of it this way Governor: you are getting to live a preview of the future life you're creating for everyone else. You get to experience it firsthand to see what life will be like when you have pre-emptively implemented unreliable sources of energy. You see yourself as this environmental warrior, a trailblazer forging the path ahead for recalcitrant souls who must be dragged into the light. You are now in a place that allows you to live out your beliefs as they are, not as you imagine they will be. You are the first to experience the results of your policies firsthand. It could be argued that you are beta-testing the new environmentally friendly future that you created to see how it works. I expect you to set a good example for the rest of us and accept it all without complaining."

"You son of a—" yelled the governor.

"Stop! Not one more word," snapped the voice. "It IS cold, so you can buy a cover to help you keep warm with your money if you want to use your pay for that purpose. You will also be able to buy new batteries when the ones you're using for your lighting eventually die out. To tell you the truth, I don't know how long those batteries will last. If I were you, I would not leave them on all the time like you're doing; the batteries are expensive to replace and not always available."

"I have $150.00 here in tens, fives, and ones," the voice said. "I'm going to count them out on this table." The voice slowly counted out the $150.00. "There, this is all yours. You worked for it. First, though, I need to take 30 percent off the 150.00 for taxes. I must have income myself, you understand, for all the good work I want to do on behalf of all my other subjects. You know, the ones that I care about? So, 30 percent of $150.00 is $45 dollars. That leaves you $105.00. The use of the cot will cost you $10. Then there's the issue of your failure to comply with my order about cleaning your area. For that infraction, there's a $25 fine."

"You can't be serious?" said the governor.

"Of course I can," retorted the voice. "I'm being lenient for a first offense. There is also the Pure Air Tax."

"What's THAT?" the governor asked.

"Well," continued the voice, "you are breathing oxygen in my realm and breathing out carbon dioxide. You are polluting my air by the fact that you're breathing. That tax is $15.00."

The governor said, "How can you charge me a tax for breathing?"

"Because I can; I'm the emperor now. You charge taxes for all sorts of pollution," the voice said. "You want people to drive less, so you put the highest gas taxes in the nation on your citizens. People still must drive to work, at least the ones who work and pay the taxes you place on them. They need to go to the store, to school, and all the other places necessary to live their daily lives with no help from you. You just charge them for the privilege. Yet, you have not prohibited drive-throughs at the thousands of restaurants and other businesses in your state. The ones that have cars lined up with their engines running, producing those emissions that you are so worried about. Unless they cannot physically do so, for the sake of the environment, should those people not go inside a restaurant or a store to order and get their products? Would not that reduce pollution? Tell me, Governor, if pollution is such an existential threat, why are traffic lights not programmed to flash red or yellow so that people are not required to sit at red lights when there's no traffic? It seems ridiculous that at night or reduced traffic times when they are at increased risk of being carjacked or robbed, people should be forced under threat of penalty to violate common sense when there's no other traffic. No, you cannot do that; there would be no tax revenue in it for you, even though it might help reduce the pollution you are so worried about. Hell, it might even reduce crime; it is harder to carjack a vehicle when it's moving than when it's sitting at a red light.

"However, to answer your question about how I can tax you for breathing," said the voice, "I am simply following the logic that you use on the gas taxes. Governor, maybe you should breathe a little slower or breathe a little less to avoid an increase in your personal Pure Air Tax."

"You asshole!" yelled the governor. "How am I supposed to do that? Breathe less, that's ridiculous."

"That's not my problem; it's your problem to solve," said the voice. "Just like it's the people's problem to solve how to get back and forth to work in their gas cars and make financial ends meet because of YOUR policies," the voice said. "Now you must deal with MY policies, MY rules. How do you like being on this end of rules that cause YOU problems?"

"I see what you're doing here," said the governor. "I'm not playing this game."

"You frustrate and amuse me at the same time, Governor," said the voice. "Let us get on with the business at hand. That leaves you a balance of $55. If you don't want the money, I have other uses for it. Remember, you have been warned. There will be consequences if you don't do what I tell you to do."

"What are the consequences if I don't take the money?" the governor asked.

"The answer is simple. Among other things, as I keep telling you, you will not eat or drink, and you may freeze to death. It is up to you. I do not care," the voice replied bluntly.

"Ok, ok! I want to buy some food, and I want something to keep me warm," the governor answered.

The voice said, "I'll be back with the items that you want." The voice left the space for what seemed like an eternity.

The governor's stomach was growling, and he started shivering almost uncontrollably. When the voice returned, he said, "There's a sandwich and some water in a paper cup being placed in your cage."

"Can't I get some bottled water?" demanded the governor.

"Oh, NO, Governor, plastics are not allowed," the voice responded. "A paper cup is what you will use. Of course, it's not very sturdy, so, at some point, you'll have to replace it, at your own expense, of course. So, treat it gently. The sandwich will be $20 dollars."

"What????" the governor said. "That's ridiculous."

"I'm shocked at your response," the voice said. "Of all people, you should certainly understand that given the increase in costs that we all are experiencing because of you and your followers, this isn't an unreasonable price. The person who sold me the sandwich said that since you raised the minimum wage so high, they had to raise their prices to make ends meet. You do realize, don't you, that the costs and taxes you place on businesses simply get passed on to the consumer? Your action would lead one to believe that you do not know that simple fact. Did you think that those small businesses could just absorb the increase? That will also be $6 for the water."

"Aww, come on, that's crazy," said the governor.

"That's the price. Take it or leave it. It is quite a bargain. Damn!" exclaimed the voice. "I should have added transportation costs to your bill on top of the base price and tax. I'll correct that mistake if there's a next time you eat here. Of course, it is a cold sandwich. I would not want to offend your environmental sensitivities by having you eat anything prepared on a stove or an oven. I'm taking $28, including tax, from your pay to cover the cost of your meal. That leaves you $27. Now, how about something to help keep you from freezing?"

"How much is that?" asked the governor.

"Oh, that item's a bargain," said the voice. "It's only $40."

"I'll take it; I'm freezing," the governor said.

"Ok, we have a deal," said the voice. "I'm taking another $44 from your pay to cover the cost, plus tax. That leaves you owing me $17."

"If you only gave me $150.00, how can you charge me those prices?" asked the governor. "You know I won't have enough to pay for them?"

"I'm not overcharging you, Governor," the voice said. "What you are now experiencing is what thousands of people in your state experience every day. It should not bother you. I'm just following your example. You just keep piling on the taxes and the fees. If it doesn't bother you, why should it bother me?"

The governor stayed silent. The next time the voice spoke, its tone had changed. "Stay where you are," the voice said. "A small slide over by your bucket will open. The items you purchase will be put inside with you. Your bucket will be taken, emptied, and returned. If you move from where you are, the items that you've paid for will be confiscated for non-compliance with my orders. Also, be aware that there is a $10 tax for solid and liquid waste disposal. I would cut down on my usage of that convenience if I were you. Your deficit is now $27, and you have a week to go until your next pay. Governor, you need to learn how to manage your money better. I must say, I am not surprised at your spending habits, given your tendency to spend exorbitantly. You should consider needing and using less. Financially, you are not off to a very good start in that regard."

The governor was annoyed. "You have NO idea how much my administration helps the citizens of this state. I don't treat them the way you say I do."

"Actually, I do know, Governor," said the voice as it put the items into the cell and locked the slide back in place. "You help a tremendous number of people who are NOT citizens, all paid for by the people who are citizens. That is like adopting children and then telling your natural children to go live in the yard, only feeding them scraps, and telling them to go get a job so that they can help you pay for your newly adopted children. You are taking our hard-earned money and giving it to your new friends. It is not your money to give, at least not until you TAKE it from us. Along that line, you might want to be thinking about how you are going to earn some money while you're here, or it's going to be a very uncomfortable existence for you."

After the items were placed in the cage, the voice instructed the governor that he could go and retrieve them. The governor reached for what he thought was going to be a sweater or a jacket and immediately dropped it on the floor. "What the hell's this?" he said.

The voice answered, "That is what will help keep you warm. We know how you feel about petroleum products and fossil fuels. We could not in good conscience provide you with something that had been produced with petroleum products. What you have in your hand is a pelt crafted by hand from a recently harvested animal. To be honest, I am shocked and surprised by your reaction. Is this not your vision of the future? How could you not like it? If there are no petroleum products, how do you think material needs like sweaters and coats are going to be produced in mass? All those things that we need and rely on daily. How are we to work? Live? Get nourishment? And keep warm while waiting on you to get the 'alternative sources of energy' online? You have been very pampered, Governor, from birth, by your rich parents, your private schools, as a lawyer, and in your high-paying government positions. Those days are gone. Get used to reaping what you have sown. This is the future you are trying to take us to while you drive around in your gas-guzzler SUV and heat the mansion with fossil fuels. Does it occur to you that others see it as hypocritical of you to make the demands that you make of your citizens when you don't even have solar panels on the governor's mansion? It is good for thee but not for me, RIGHT!?"

The governor reluctantly wrapped the pelt around him, went over, picked up the sandwich, and started eating.

The voice continued, "Actually, Governor, you're lucky you're being subjected to my rules here instead of yours. Think of all the other taxes you are not paying. You do not have a car here, so I can't charge you all the taxes you impose on cars, like gas, fees, and excise taxes on insurance. You do the same thing to homeowners," the voice continued. "You put a surcharge on house insurance to prevent mortgage lenders from losing money on loans to people who, perhaps, should not get loans in the first place. You use the surcharge to feed your funds to help them offset the down payment and mortgages. You don't give THAT privilege to ALL your citizens, do you? You put that cost on homeowners who are already trying to pay for their own loans and others who cannot afford a house themselves. Now, under you, they must support someone else too. You are taking your piece off all those surcharges and putting their money into your fund to support your wealth transfer plans. Just like your friends are doing on the national level, making taxpayers pay for someone else's school loans. That was another very clever little sleight of hand you pulled off there, but I am your emperor now. I will enjoy levying more taxes and fees on you."

The governor took the last bite of the sandwich. As the voice's footsteps started to fade into the distance, it said, "It just occurred to me that maybe I will tax you because you don't have those things to tax. YES! That is what I will do. After I have exhausted all the ways I can think of to tax, fee, or fine you, I'll tax you for not having anything left for me to tax. I like that idea. It is like you want to tax our savings and tax our investments for unrealized gains. Just thinking of that plan of yours inspires me to come up with even more diabolical ways to make you pay for your behaviors."

"Screw you!" yelled the governor. "We're doing what needs to be done and should have been done a long time ago."

The voice, irritated by the governor's reaction, continued, "We understand your version of logic, Governor; your logic is ideologically deep but intellectually shallow. Under your dictatorial version of leadership, we see you as wanting us to cut off everything now and sacrifice people's lives in the name of environmentalism and equality. YOU THINK you'll be providing us with a future life out of a science fiction movie where every problem of mankind has been solved. WE THINK that the more likely scenario is that, under your leadership, we will wind up living like the Flintstones, walking everywhere, hanging our laundry on a line outside, regardless of the weather, and all of us having a scheduled time to cook, based upon when our ration of electricity will be turned on so that we CAN cook."

The governor said, "I've listened to you. I don't agree with you. You're delusional and misinformed. Ok, I guess I can see how some people may see it the way you are, but they don't know what I know or see the information I have. I really do believe we're in crisis. I believe I must act; I'm the governor, and I have a lot of people who believe the same things I do."

The voice said, "We DO believe that YOU think we're in crisis. People have been saying that for fifty years, and a tremendous amount of improvement has been made and is continuing to be made, but it's against your 'sky is falling' narrative to recognize how much has been accomplished. That would not fit your agenda, would it?

"What is sad," the voice went on, "and disappointing, is that most people do want a better and cleaner future. We understand there are climate issues. The main problem for us is that you all have lost the confidence of just about everyone but the extremists and the leftists of all varieties, them and those who want to see this country destroyed. Politicians have generally had a very low credibility rating, but you people have taken it to a new low. You've even contaminated science with your political agenda so badly that the average person cannot trust even what scientists say."

"That's not true. We MUST prevent misinformation. What we're doing is too important to be sidetracked by people who don't understand or are just plain ignorant," spewed the governor.

The voice said, "We all have read and heard about the scientists who can't get published because they have data that challenges yours. Let me clarify that: those of us who don't solely get their news from your controlled media outlets have read and heard about them. You have the tech and social media companies that block and censor information and discussions that might challenge your thinking. What are you afraid of, Governor? That is how science is supposed to work. Explore, experiment, challenge the findings, and keep working on the data and the information to come up with the best answer, not just the answer you want. The actions of you and those who think like you keep creating your own problems with your messages and your actions. There is a very large population that does not trust the government or anything it says, and that population is growing every day.

"Not everyone who disagrees with your experts is ignorant," said the voice. "Instead of trying to improve the information or engage in the discussion, you shut it down and decide what you will allow to be published because it meets your agenda. NOTHING in science gets accepted as fact without argument, more studies, conflicting results, more studies, and eventually general acceptance. But not your experts: they know all, and they must not be challenged. You said it yourself; anyone who disagrees with you either does not understand or is ignorant. More honesty and allowing the opposing expert views to be argued unfiltered by your media friends in public may help your causes rather than harm them. Quit putting people in separate camps. Give them proposals that bring them together. Ones that make sense to them and can be supported.

"You follow the same pattern in everything you touch," said the voice, "not just the environment: in crime, the justice system, education, healthcare, immigration, homelessness, everything important to everyone. You have screwed it all up, maybe beyond repair. You should have engaged with and tried some of the solutions from people who don't agree with you or think the way you all do. You may have been surprised at the results.

"Power," said the voice, "is your main objective! Total control because you are so smart, and the rest of us must be dragged by the hair on our heads or our shirt collars, kicking and screaming, into your future for our own good. You turn our lives over to regulatory agencies filled with philosophical ideologues and push ridiculous solutions to non-existent problems down our throats. Nobody but you and your liberal elitists believe that what you are doing is going to solve the problems the way you're going about it with your edicts and decrees. Your solutions have as many issues as the problems you're trying to solve. You are costing us our future and our kids' future while you claim to be fighting for them. You tax us to signal your righteousness and use the money to buy votes and try to outdo each other in a competition to see who can destroy what was once a shining example of a working democracy. Simply because this country has not yet become what YOU think it should be by now. You are willing to tax the taxpayers into poverty with your taxes and wealth transfer schemes. All the while saying you are fighting poverty. You are willing to sacrifice individuals and families who have worked hard to obtain what they have, along with their dreams, their safety, and security, to satisfy your own ego. Yet, you kiss the ass of foreign polluters and praise their false efforts to control their own pollution. They are adding coal-powered power plants every other day, Governor, and you know they are. Where is your public outcry and condemnation over what they are doing?"

"We're not destroying this country," the governor said, his voice rising with the passion of the true believer. "We are making it better, better for everyone. It's the turn of those, the people who have not benefited from the years of oppressing others, to receive from the wealth of this society."

"But," said the voice, "one of the problems with your solutions is that the ones you're punishing have done none of the things for which you have found them guilty."

"It doesn't matter whether they're guilty or not," said the governor. "They've benefited from the past."

"And not all the ones you're giving money and privilege to," said the voice, "have contributed anything to this country in any way, and several are here to make it worse intentionally."

The governor grunted his disagreement and walked to the other side of his cage, away from the voice. He held up his empty water cup and asked, "Could I have a refill?"

"Sure," the voice said, "it'll cost you $6 plus tax."

"But I need water," the governor said.

"Yeah, a lot of people need things. A lot more people are going to need things when you get done with your agenda. I guess you are just one person more now who can join that group."

The governor said, "You've misjudged me. I'm just trying to do the best I can for the people who elected me. I have a family, too. I'm concerned about my own kid's future. I want to make it the best one for them that I can."

The voice said, "You should have opened your eyes and realized that's part of the problem. You're doing the best you can for the people who elected you and people like you. But there are almost as many people who live in your state that did not vote for you or don't have all the monied opportunities you grew up with or that your kids are growing up with, and, contrary to your beliefs, they're not all minorities. Under the old rules of the society that you loathe, you were their governor, too. But you changed all that. Those who didn't vote for you or do not agree with you are the enemy to be ignored and punished. They only exist to meet your goals and your needs. In the position you hold, you are supposed to LEAD, not be a dictator. That, again, is why you are contemptuously called the emperor. If you truly represented all people in this state, you would not be here with me."

"What do you mean?" said the governor. "What I've done works. I've been re-elected multiple times."

"AND YET, HERE you are!" said the voice. "Maybe you should have worked more to gain consensus and move forward with as much support as your leadership skills could attract. Educate, listen, collaborate, and trade ideas and solutions. No, that would have required work and patience. You have the majority in both houses, so you just ram your agenda items through because you think you're smarter than the rest of us. You don't recognize any wisdom but your own."

The governor said, "But we do NOT have time to educate and bring people along who don't understand the importance of what we're doing. We're running out of time. We've reached the point of environmental collapse if we don't act now."

"Yeah, I heard you use that statement," said the voice, "and I don't believe that even YOU really believe that. Even if you and your colleagues in other states and DC could do everything you want, it would make a much smaller difference to the planet than you're so assured it will. Your state's worldwide environmental impact on the planet is almost negligible. It's one of the three least-polluting states in this country. While you sacrifice your citizens for your future career and ideologies, the other major polluters in the world are doing way more damage than the US. On that subject, you and your friends are silent.

"Have you ever heard of 'change management'?" asked the voice.

"Of course, I've heard of it," said the governor.

"Well, you really suck at it," said the voice.

The governor stood up and walked toward the voice, saying, "But we have to DO SOMETHING, show leadership, point the way."

The voice said, "I understand that. I even agree with it. The problem is that you create mandates to signal how serious you are. You consider THAT leadership. You do have a vision in mind, even if part of it is hallucination. One of your critics publicly called it "your fantasy." If you had a detailed, well-thought-out transition plan with a timeline that could be realistically funded and managed with a reasonable schedule, you might have a lot more people following you. Maybe you and your like-minded governors and legislators should have banded together and lectured and educated the leaders of the high-polluting countries in the world instead of kissing their asses and giving THEM a pass. Maybe let some of THEIR citizens feel the burden of saving the planet. You might have at least a bit more credibility."

"But we do have a plan," said the governor.

The voice laughed and said, "You're keeping it a very good secret. If the next thing you tell me is that not allowing the sale of gas-powered vehicles beyond 2035 is THE PLAN, your next few hours and days are going to be extremely difficult for you. From what I see, you have a lot of goals, but your planning and execution of that plan are a disaster in the making. Of course, you can pass your laws saying that no fossil-fueled cars can be sold in this state. And I guess you can enforce that, but to what end? Does that sound like leadership to you? Your plan was called a fantasy because, among other reasons, there is no real plan to make a smooth transition. You just drove a stake in the ground and hoped that someone comes up with a way to make it true. Why? Because you could. You believe that because you say it shall be done, that it will be done! What if your plan doesn't work? Are you really prepared to shut down a state and its economy because you think the good fairy is going to wave a magic wand and make your wishes come true?"

The voice continued, "What is your transition plan timeline to bring charging stations online as you force gas stations out of business? Where do the lines on the graphs cross that are guiding your decisions? If you wipe out gas stations before you have enough electric generation capacity and charging capability, what happens then? Do you even know what the needed capacity will be? Hasn't it been determined, once again, that your projections of the energy requirements of your state have been woefully underestimated? The people in your state receive notices now from the power company not to operate electrical appliances when the temperature drops or rises because the electrical systems are stretched to their maximum. What is the timeline for the added capacity? You do nothing to adjust your timelines in the face of those realities. Not that I necessarily agree, but maybe if you had included hybrid vehicles in your thinking, which use both gas and electric motors, you could have bought some time, and you could have had a better chance at making a transition possible that people could have lived with. At least for now. Electric cars do not have the mileage range to sustain a modern lifestyle. Most people who have one will tell you that unless you have a gas-powered car as a backup or an alternative, you are limited in what you can do and where you can go. Are you hoping that with your social policies, taxes, and regulations, you will force enough people to leave your state and make up for the gap between demand and capacity?"

"It's very rare that the power companies put out those notices," said the governor. "We also have plans in the pipeline to introduce new energy sources."

The voice laughed. "It's ironic that you use the word 'pipeline.' I thought that would be included on your 'forbidden words to use' list. It may be rare, Governor, but every time one of those notices goes out, it calls into doubt the very questions that I'm asking and weakens support for your plan. Communities in your state have rejected proposals for windmills and other green projects. Unless I'm misinformed, you and your staff of alarmist environmentalists have directed your agencies to ignore environmental impact statements that go against your proposals. Everyone who has two brain cells to rub together knows power blackouts and brownouts will be a part of their future under your plans. How are you going to meet the infrastructure needs by the deadlines you've set? How much more in taxes are you going to pile on people to pay for it? More taxes, higher utility bills, and less efficient everything. At what costs, Governor? At what cost? You know, as sure as you stand there, you're planning astronomical electric rate increases to be placed on the electrical energy users in this state. People are going to be paying a lot more to light and heat their homes. What about those people who cannot afford those increases to their housing budget? What about the people who cannot afford electric cars or replacement cars for the car they have now? What about the people who cannot afford any car now, even a used car that runs on gas, let alone an electric one? What will you do about them?"

"The state will help them make the transition," said the governor.

"Oh, REALLY? How are you going to help them?" asked the voice. "Are you going to tax them more to pay for the help they will need?"

"Yes, it's true," said the governor. "Taxes will need to be increased to help those who need it to transition, and yes, there will need to be increases in the cost of electric utilities. Sacrifices must be made. There is no other way to do it."

The voice said, "You DO KNOW your plan's going to put a lot more people from the middle-earner group into the low-earner group, including several who could wind up in the homeless camp, don't you?"

"Well, as I said," said the governor, "sacrifices will have to be made. Those who CAN pay will need to pay even more to help those who cannot. There's no getting around that. It's just reality."

"Have you thought about the fact that you are making their current gas-powered vehicles worthless? Have you?" challenged the voice. "What are they going to do with their worthless gas-powered cars: convert them into planters for the vegetable gardens they are going to need or sell them for scrap? WHAT IS YOUR PLAN? HOW MUCH IS IT GOING TO COST? You keep preaching about what needs to be done to save us all, but you don't talk about what those sacrifices are, and you're not saying who exactly is going to be doing the sacrificing! Governor, a lot of the people that are trusting and following you are going to be very surprised when they learn it will be THEM doing the sacrificing."

"I'm sure reasonable people know societal and economic shifts of this significance cannot be made without some pain and changes to the status quo," the governor said.

"So, let me get this straight," said the voice. "You are going to shift your entire state off fossil fuels and reduce poverty at the same time? Is that what I'm hearing?"

"Yes, that's true. We believe we can manage it," said the governor.

"How can you believe that?" asked the voice. "Government does not produce a product for profit. If the competitive marketplace and private enterprise are not financing this massive change in the time you have dictated, the only way that the government can raise money for those changes you're talking about is to raise taxes and increase utility costs. You sure as hell won't cut any current spending to provide the money for all that you want to do. Please explain it to me. WHO IS MANAGING this significant 'shift show'?" the voice asked. "Show the people the data, the real data. Show us the plan. Show us the milestones to be met and the dates they are to be met. Show us who is going to pay for all of this. Tell us who is accountable for each part of the plan. Tell us, who are you going to hold accountable for developing and managing the plan, Governor? A private enterprise created an electric car and installed a network of charging stations nationwide to support their cars. The national government allocated half a billion dollars several years ago to start building a charging station network, and, after years, the government has only installed a total number of charging stations that can be counted on two hands. Where will the money that was allocated for that infrastructure project disappear to before it's applied for its intended purpose? At the current installation rate, you won't meet your own deadlines. As time passes, government inefficiency, government raiding of the funds, and inflation will consume the allocated resources. Of course, then more tax money will be needed."

"In my state, we have a plan; it has been published; we're not hiding it," said the governor.

"I have seen your high-level aspirations and wishful targets but have not seen your detailed plan for the transition away from fossil fuel that has held up to the force of reality. What we are seeing is what won't be allowed under your laws and regulatory dictates.

"I've also seen what you have published about your plan to reduce poverty, Governor," said the voice. "I would say that it is full of what you intend to do in very veiled terms with statement like 'transition to... and provide for...' Your estimates of the cost ranges are documented like a restaurant menu price review with one-to-three-dollar sign symbols. You do not give total prices or specifics for any of it, but from seeing all the three-dollar sign symbols, I can tell you it is going to take a lot of tax increases. You have not shared the bottom-line amount of dollars you expect to get through taxes and spend over the next ten years, have you? You will be very busy taking money from one segment of the population and giving it to another. At the same time you're doing that, you're planning on significantly increasing their utility bills, adding taxes to pay for the infrastructure and your other projects, along with your other dictates that are going to cost the taxpaying citizens even more. A large population of those people in the middle who are simply trying to make ends meet, as we speak, will just fall further down the economic scale under your plans. Even your supporters are going to lose their enthusiasm when they realize what it's going to do to them personally."

"I'm sure they'll be more supportive than you think," said the governor. "Unlike you, they know how important what we're doing is to level the economic, social, and environmental playing fields."

The voice said, "Well when they are on the receiving end of paying for what you're doing, I wouldn't be surprised to see a few politicians being chased down the streets of the Capital by people with pitchforks. But that is for you folks to worry about. Have you ever thought of basing your schedules on affordability, capability, and reality rather than hopeful guesses? You have spent millions on poverty and homelessness already. Where is the data that says any of the money you've spent has made a significant difference? All you report is that there are 'Bright Spots.' You were elected to lead! Part of that is making sure there is a plan that's tracked and managed and, most importantly, that the plan is working. You should have been keeping the data and progress information in front of the public regularly. WARTS and all, not hiding the reality. If objectives or targets are not being met, then admit it and deal with it," said the voice. "Look at your assumptions and question what's not working before you just keep throwing more money at a problem that's not getting better. Get some other ideas about what the problem is and how to fix it."

"I think you're being over dramatic," said the governor smugly. "We think we have a plan that will work and provide the outcomes we desire."

The voice said, "Governor, I do not, for a second, believe you and your compatriots are telling the truth about your plans. Yes, I believe your objectives are real, but I more firmly believe that you are purposefully lying to the citizens of your state about how the result will look for them. Sure, it may be better for some small portion of the population, and I'm not at all sure about that. You cannot realistically achieve all that you're trying to do in the time you're saying you will without serious detriment to a large portion of the population: the ones who will pay for it. It simply isn't possible."

The governor, in full chest-puffing arrogance, snapped back at the voice, "That's why I AM the governor, and you're just a disembodied voice afraid to show your face. It doesn't matter what you think. We'll achieve what we say, regardless of the costs."

"Then, Governor, I will make sure YOU pay a price of MY choosing. My advice to you, Governor, is to think long and hard about what you just said to me and ask what YOU are willing to sacrifice to get what you want.

"We're done for now," said the voice. "I'm going to leave you with this. You, who, in your arrogance, does not listen to anyone but your own echo chamber, is going to have the opportunity to hear some people discussing you and your friend's policies. The people that you will hear are people who do not agree with you, and neither are they people to whom you would normally listen. For your listening pleasure, we will be providing recordings of previously broadcast programs. You will find perspectives from experts other than yours, along with the stories and comments of regular citizens discussing your sacred programs and their impact on their lives. These people represent different views than those that you hold so dear. It's about time you heard them."

With those comments, a speaker located somewhere outside the cage came to life, "Today we're going to talk about the governor's plan for the near-term elimination of fossil fuels; our number is 555—OUR—TURN if you'd like to call into the program today…"

"Wait!" the governor replied. "I want to explain more."

The voice said, "We're done!" And then there was silence except for the voices from the speaker.

The governor tried to shut out the sound coming from the speaker. Unable to ignore what the talkers were saying, he began arguing with their uninterruptable positions. The speaker continued without commercials. Hammering home their opinions. Exhausting one topic and beginning another. Each subject dissected by the host of the show, his guests, and the people calling in to the program, giving their opinions or making comments. The governor lectured right back at them about how they were all wrong. Telling those voices that if they were not so ignorant, they would see that he was right to be doing the things that he and his friends in other states and at the national level were doing. The issues discussed were part of the governor's overall agenda. He wished that he had called into the program when it aired so he could set them straight.

The governor, facing the direction the speaker seemed to be coming from, realized the futility of arguing with a piece of electronic gear. It was not a person. He could not talk over it the way he could talk over a real person. The governor shook his head, walked slowly over to the cot, and sat down, placing his elbows on his knees, and lowering his head into his hands. The voices from the speaker continued without a break.

The hunger and the cold were now constant. *How the hell did this happen?* He thought. *I have security for myself, my family, and my home. I have a 24/7 security detail. And here I am, not sure what's going to happen to me or even whether I'll ever see my family again.* The anger and frustration rising in him overflowed. He rose from the cot and crossed the cage to the closest bars, grabbed them with both hands, and shook them as hard as he could. He assumed he was being watched and screamed in desperation at the air toward where the voice usually came from. "I will be found, and you'll pay for what you've done to me." Shaking the bars again and swearing at his situation, he let go of the bars and returned to the cot. He was tired, hungry, cold, and seriously pissed off.

Hours passed, and the recordings that had been playing continuously on so many subjects that he had lost track suddenly stopped, and a different voice spoke. This one in person and close by. "Listen to me," it said. "I have someone with me. They have a gun, and it's pointed at you. Do as I tell you, and you won't get hurt. Do you understand? Another little protest like the one you gave a little while ago and your gentle treatment here could go in another direction. A direction that you will not like."

The governor looked around nervously and said, "Yes, I understand."

The new voice said, "Good; now get up off the cot and move over by the food door. Turn around, away from the main door. Stay there and don't move. Do it now. If you do anything other than what I've told you, it will hurt. You've been warned."

The governor did what he was told. He could hear the door open and footsteps and a scraping sound. The footsteps sounded again, and the door closed. The new voice said, "We're done here. Count to five, and then you can turn around."

The governor counted to five and slowly turned around. There was no one there, but the cot was gone. He sat down against the bars with his head in his hands until he lay down and fell asleep on the cold floor. The sound of a voice woke him. "How was your sleep?" the voice asked.

"Not good. I'm cold, I'm hungry, and now I have nothing to sit or lie on but a cold, hard floor."

"Yeah, someone else decided they needed that cot more than you did, so they took it," the voice said. "But you understand that, right? Property rights are kind of a thing of the past, as you know. Just because you paid for it and had possession of it doesn't mean it really belongs to you when someone else needs it or just wants it. RIGHT?"

"What are you talking about?" asked the governor.

The voice answered, "Well, it's kind of like someone having a car so that they can get to work, go to school, transport the family, and all the other things you do with a car. Then along comes someone who decides they don't want to work for the things they want. They decide they will just take what belongs to someone else. Someone who worked for it. You apparently don't see that as a crime anymore. Burglaries in your state are twice the national average. You let people steal with impunity. Those are just statistics to you, correct? But the family who had their car stolen now has no transportation. How do they get to work? To school? To the doctor? Now, because of you and your policies, they may have to pay off a car they no longer have, or that has been destroyed, or get a lot less than it's worth from an insurance company. Then, they must buy another vehicle to replace the one that was stolen. On top of that, their insurance rates are going to go up. But hey, you know, Governor, we cannot just keep locking these same people up. What is it you say? We must break the cycle. Because the thieves stealing those vehicles are victims, too? In the old west, horse thieves were hung because they'd stolen a vital piece of survival. Just like a car is a vital piece of survival to people today. What are they supposed to do without their car? WHY are YOU letting this happen? Mister Former Emperor, think about how you have been serving your citizens! You sure ARE serving SOME segments, but not all of them. It looks like you are punishing hard-working people with taxes and other penalties.

Pushing them into poverty while allowing criminals to assist you in victimizing your citizens as part of your wealth transfer program. It could be viewed as a partnership between you and the criminals intended to do as much damage to your law-abiding citizens as possible. Then, on top of all that, if those same citizens try to protect themselves, you make criminals out of the people you should be protecting and serving. You and your twisted logic create paradoxes where none should exist."

The governor stood up and said, "Look, you idiot, you don't understand. We're fighting against racism and poverty and for the dignity of an underserved and mistreated population. It's been a national and international disgrace the way these people have been treated."

"But, Governor," said the voice, "a lot of the car thieves are teenage white males and females, not just minorities. What is your reason for letting that go on? What social justice correction is being served in those cases? Did you ever think about maybe banning *Grand Theft Auto*, which may be their inspiration, while you are busy banning stoves, furnaces, air conditioners, guns, and fossil fuels?"

The governor said, "I've had enough of this. I want out of here, and I want out of here now! I will be found, and you'll be the one in jail. So do yourself a favor and let me go. I can help you if you let me go now. I'll tell them I wasn't harmed."

The voice went silent, the familiar footsteps fading away.

The sound of voices from the speaker broke the silence. "Today's topic is rampant crime, what's happening, and what's not being done about it? In fact, we'll discuss how crime is being incentivized by the politicians, prosecutors, and judges who are supposed to protect us, the public. We'll have two victims on later in the program to tell of their experiences as victims of crimes. One is a small store owner who has closed his business because of repeated robberies and a lack of support from law enforcement, prosecutors, judges, and his elected officials. The other has been labeled a criminal by the prosecutor's office when he fought back after being attacked and beaten in his own front yard. Our number is 555—OUR—TURN if you would like to call into the show today..."

The governor placed his hands over his ears, but the volume simply increased. This time, he didn't argue out loud. He knew it would be useless and a waste of his already weakening vitality. This time, he lay on the cold floor, hoping the voices coming from the speaker would eventually turn into background noise and allow him some sleep. When that did not happen, he lay quietly and worked to take apart the points being made coming from the speaker. Imagining himself in a courtroom representing himself against his opponents. He did have to admit that the host and the guests scored some points occasionally. He also found the audience of the program told some stories that could register very sympathetically to a jury made up of average citizens who were not hand-picked by himself and his cohorts. Eventually, he gratefully felt the relief of sleep overtaking him.

He had no idea how long or how little he had been asleep when the voice said, "I think I may have your attention now. At least you realize you are being treated the same way you treat other people, good people, by most standards, but not yours. You don't like being treated the way you treat them, do you? That's too bad, satisfying for me, but too bad for you!

"Regarding your earlier comments, as for you being found, I'm not sure you ever will be found. If you are, it will be because I want you found. If you don't go back, things might be better for a lot of people. Your disappearance could be a very strong message about what happens to dictators and self-appointed emperors. So, yes, I'm ok with the risk of what could happen to just me. I could do a lot of good for some segments of humanity by just keeping you here where you can't do any more harm."

"You arrogant son of a bitch! You're going to regret this," spewed the governor. "I have an entire police force working for me. The FBI will be after you. None of you involved in this will get away with any of this. When you're caught, it'll be the trial of the century. Because of what you've done, kidnapping a sitting governor, you'll just prove how radical you are. Because of you, we'll be able to enact new laws that ensure your voice and your followers will never win another election."

The voice did not reply.

The speaker started again. "On today's program, we're going to talk with three guests. Two are a couple, and the third is a single mother. While faced with different circumstances, all are being forced to move from their homes. One is a retired couple selling their house because the property taxes on their home exceeded their mortgage payment, and looking at upgrading their home to meet all the new green programs would be more than they could afford on their fixed incomes. Combined with those fears, they're concerned they will not be able to pay the upcoming increased utility rates arising from the elimination of natural gas as a source of energy that their house uses currently. Their intent is to move to another less oppressive and expensive state. The single mother's rent has been raised twice since she moved in, and her landlords have decided to sell her rental home to one of the big companies buying up single-dwelling homes, raising the prices, and re-renting them for more money. Our number is…"

Much later, when the voice returned. The speaker stopped, and the voice said, "I've been listening to you. You still seem to think you're justified in all that you do. So, we have a problem, you, and me. Well, just YOU have a problem. I'm willing to sacrifice myself for the greater good as I see it. Besides, it looks to us like, and I will add, it looks the same to one of your political strategists," continued the voice, "that if nothing changes, people who think as I do will never win another election anyway. You already have 'the elections locked up for the foreseeable future,' I believe was the quote I read from him."

"What is it you want from me?" the governor demanded.

"What do YOU think I want from you," the voice said.

"I don't know, is there a ransom?" answered the governor. "Maybe you just want to be famous to your friends for kidnapping or killing someone who's trying to do some things you're too stupid to understand."

The voice said, "See, there YOU go again! You have learned nothing from our talks. You still believe you are the be-all and end-all, the font of all knowledge. But you don't even know what it takes to really lead. You can get those who believe like you do to follow you. But, listening to you, I'm beginning to wonder if it's YOU leading THEM, or THEM, your elitist and radical friends, leading YOU? Are you just doing what they want so you can be their hero or stay in office? You don't even recognize that there are others, others who are just as smart but see the problems and the solutions differently than you. You don't involve them in your committees and task forces. Is THEIR way of thinking not to be considered in any way? You just said to me that I don't understand. I believe I do understand. But in your worldview, anyone who disagrees with you is supposed to shut up, sit back, and bask in the light of your superior intelligence? It is sad that you don't consider other points of view to reach possible paths forward... together. A path that could potentially engage many more people, leading to more workable solutions, or at least solutions that they had a part in developing. That might be an easier road for everyone to be on. YOU need to think about whether YOUR path is the only path, the path that YOU want to follow to death, without even questioning the wisdom of your own approach and processes."

"I want to know something," said the governor. "Are those programs you are playing while you are not here real or scripted for my benefit?

"They are real stories. You wouldn't know it, but they have been on various media. None that you would pay attention to."

"So, you're telling me that the people they interview are real also and that the stories they tell are true."

"Yes, they are. If you'd ever chosen to listen to some different perspectives, you would have heard some of them yourself. You can decide for yourself if you were out of touch with those people or if you simply did not care about them."

With the sound of footsteps receding away, the voice said, "I'm going to leave you alone for a while and let you think about all we've talked about. I want you to think about what got you here in the first place. Think about why I have spent this much time over you and taken such a risk. Ask yourself why you are still here. NOT dead, but still here? Even if we released you, you must realize we can get you back anytime we want to. Why would we even go to all this trouble when, if we wanted you dead, you could have been killed at any time? Take your time, Governor; I'll be back."

"Wait! WAIT!" said the governor, "I'm hungry; I need something to eat."

"You don't have any money left," said the voice. "In fact, you owe me money. But that's not my problem, Governor; you had taxes and fees to pay TO ME! YOUR emperor. I can guess what your attitude was when you were in charge. You would probably say something like, 'Give to Caesar what is Caesar's,' you thinking you were Caesar and all. Well, you USED to be Caesar. So, I followed your leadership example. Whatever I demand of you, you will give it to me, or else! Thank you very much.

"Oh, before I leave, have you thought about how you are going to earn money? The money to pay for what you need until next payday?"

The governor said, "I figure I don't have to because I'm guessing you already have something in mind."

"There you go again," said the voice, "always knowing the answer and knowing more than anyone else. I guess it would be appropriate if you took that opinion of yourself to the grave, especially if that is what puts you in it. I may see you later," the voice said as it faded away in the distance.

The speaker once again began, "On today's program, we're going to discuss the immigration issue. It's estimated that well over ten million people in just the last three and a half years have been welcomed into this country by the current administration. None of them have been properly vetted for security purposes. A large portion of them are military-age males. The estimated costs of these new dependents are reported to be four hundred and fifty billion dollars per year to the American taxpayer. This state alone has welcomed over four hundred thousand of those immigrants. Veterans benefits and health care have been compromised to support the influx of these people. We're being told that Social Security and Medicare will be out of money in a few years. We apparently have enough money to support the population of over three states' worth of new beneficiaries with income, health care, housing, and education but not enough to honor the commitment to social security that so many American citizens have paid for their entire working lives and rely on as income. This government will just keep raising your taxes to pay for the illegals on top of this administration's green agenda and poverty reduction program costs. This government does not care about you, the taxpayer. You are simply a vehicle to pay for the votes they're going to get from their new illegal voters. Your only role, my fellow citizens, is to pay for this administration's unlimited and out-of-control spending.

"Later in the program, we'll talk to people who've been displaced from their housing to provide shelter for the immigrants. We'll also talk to a woman who was attacked by an immigrant here illegally after escaping from justice for a similar crime in his home country. He attacked another woman in another state before coming here and attacking our guest. The perpetrator? He's still here, out of jail, and untouchable by the authorities. Our number is 555—OUR—TURN if you'd like to call in to the program today…"

The governor sat on the floor near the bars where the cot used to be and pulled the pelt around him. He was cold, his fingers stiff and red. His head hurt, he assumed from the hunger. When he had shaken the bars, he had felt his own lack of strength. His clothes were dirty, and the smell of his own urine hung in the cage. He laid down to try to sleep. He wasn't sure how long he had been awake or how long it had been since he had been taken. Sleep was the only solace he had. The speaker was his constant companion, making sleep almost impossible until exhaustion would mercifully take over and allow him to begin to drift off.

But sleep came and went. He lost track of whether minutes or hours had passed. Awake again, the speaker interviewed the woman who had been attacked by the illegal. It was a sad story. He thought of his own wife and what something like that happening to her would do to her. Not only to her but to him and their kids. But again, he thought, attacks like that committed by illegal immigrants are reasonably rare. Not all immigrants are bad people like his opposition tries to make everyone believe.

He wished he had an off switch for the speaker. He looked around the cage for a means of escape, but he still did not see one. He was stuck. He was at the mercy of some kind of zealot or group of zealots. Using that description of his captor gave him pause.

It was true the voice was breaking so many laws that the governor couldn't help but think of him as a criminal. But he had not been hurt, at least not yet. It made the governor wonder if the voice would consider himself a criminal. *Probably not; he thinks what he's doing is justified.* Another pause. *Just like me, according to the voice. I think everything that I'm doing is justified.* The voice would probably say that their followers were the more law-abiding people, more law-abiding than all the people out robbing, rioting, burning, looting, assaulting, and stealing cars. He knew from the voice how his supporters felt about those criminals and, therefore, what they thought of him and his supporters. It was not the first time the governor had heard the criticism that even if those criminals were caught, they would be released to do it all over again. *Those are people breaking the law, too. The judges and prosecutors are releasing them to do it over and over again. Those are the people who the voice and his followers see me supporting.*

*But the voice IS a criminal,* the governor thought. *He kidnapped me! I'm the governor, damn it, not just some ordinary citizen. I SHOULD be considered more important than an ordinary citizen. After all, an attack on me is an attack on the very foundation of our country and our govern-ment. Pause. But the voice would probably say that I'm no better than an ordinary citizen. An ordinary citizen just wants themselves and their family to be safe, just like I do.*

*Here I am, the governor with armed security 24/7, and here I sit in a cage. I can see how maybe some folks don't feel very safe in these times. If this happened to me, how can they feel safe? I can see why they might not be very sympathetic to my situation when crimes are being committed against ordinary citizens all over the state every single day.*

*I guess I can see how they WOULD feel more violated than I do*, the governor thought, as he laid down on the cold floor, trying to find a position that didn't hurt and allowed the pelt to cover as much of him as possible. *At least I know the floor's clean*, he chuckled to himself. He lay down on the cold floor. As he lay there, he purposefully tried not to think about all the things the voice told him that he needed to think about. He had become somewhat used to the speaker. Even though it was constant, he now considered it background noise when he focused on his own thoughts.

He turned his attention to trying to determine the purpose that this person or group that was holding him would have for doing what they were doing. What would it mean for his chance of survival or a possibility of escape? He was disappointed that he had not been found yet. He would make these folks pay, regardless of how many of them there were. He would have them hunted down and thrown in jail for the rest of their lives. As those thoughts went through his mind, he wondered if that was what they thought they had done to him. *Hunted me down and put me in jail for the rest of my life for the crimes they think I've committed?*

*Oh shit, maybe that's what's going on here.* He could feel the fear rising in him as he thought about the possibility of spending what-ever was going to be the rest of his life here in this cage. *Maybe they'll put me on trial where they're both prosecutor and judge, and I'm my only defense?* He was near panic as he thought about the voice chastising him about his arrogance, about him being the emperor. The voice had said that as governor, he didn't give a damn about anybody but himself and his supporters. The governor told himself that what the voice said was not true and that he did care about people. The ones who needed him most needed saving from themselves and saving from a society that didn't value them.

Had he been too zealous, too arrogant, or too elitist in his approach? He realized that it would not matter what he thought if he was going to be judged by a group that didn't see the world the way he saw it. It would be him who now would be judged at the mercy of THIS Emperor and THOSE supporters.

He alternated between lying awake and pacing the small area of his cage. The only plan he could come up with was to try to negotiate with the voice. Maybe he should recognize some of their arguments, whether he meant it or not, to placate them. Some of the points the voice had made had some merit, and the stories he was hearing, if true, were a growing source of concern for him. What was really happening to people that he was hearing on those programs? Maybe he wasn't as great a leader as he had thought he was. After all, it is easy to lead people who think like you do and want the exact same things that you do. It is a lot harder to get people to follow you who have other ideas about what the problems are and what needs to be done to fix them. After all, that was why slow, forced deliberate discussion, collaboration, and compromise that allowed opposing voices to be heard was built into the founding documents. The country was designed for people to work together and respect other opinions, and their right to voice them. The government was supposed to be "by the people, for the people," not a dictatorship or empire.

His mind wandered to some past leaders from history, such as George Washington, Abraham Lincoln, Franklin Roosevelt, John Kennedy, and Martin Luther King. They all had multiple constituencies that held radically different views, yet each one of those people had a vision of what could be. They brought different ideas and methods united under one roof, working together for a desired end. If those leaders had not listened, compromised, and been flexible, none of them would have moved their vision forward. *Yes, it could have been done faster if they had my authority...* That word, authority, stopped him mid-thought. Those people who had once been national and international heroes had authority, but they were not emperors. They were either elected or raised by their people to lead them, either by position, influence, or both. None were dictators or emperors because they could not be. The nation's founders, the constitution, along with human decency and respect for the citizens of this country, guided those leaders through some of the darkest times this country has seen.

* * *

The governor was startled by the sound of the voice. "It doesn't appear that you've slept much since you've been here."

"No, I guess I haven't. These are not the accommodations I'm accustomed to," replied the governor.

"Get used to it. It's the future you and your kind are forcing on the rest of us and yourselves because of your arrogance and your unrealistic plans," the voice said. "Governor, you are out of money. However, I can give you credit with a high interest if you want to buy something to eat. But first—"

The governor interrupted the voice mid-sentence, "What do you intend to do with me? I mean, you could kill me and be done with me? Or you could keep me here and keep punishing me for what you see as my sins? I don't see how either of those options serves a purpose that would cause you to go to all this trouble and risk. So, what's the plan?"

"Well, listen to you," said the voice, "asking sensible questions instead of telling me what's going to happen if I don't release you. Before you so rudely interrupted me, I was going to discuss your financial, work, and food situations. Have you thought of what work you could perform to earn what you need?"

"NO! I'm not going to play your game. I'm not going to do anything."

"Ok," said the voice, "I thought you might make that decision."

The governor heard the slide door open and saw a cloth being placed on the floor. Looking toward where he had last heard the voice, the governor asked, "What's that for?"

The voice said, "Use that cloth to clean each individual bar surrounding you. When you're done, I'll be back, and we can discuss your questions and see what can be done about your food situation."

"I won't do it," said the governor. "You can't make me."

"NO! You're PARTLY correct; I won't make you. I could, but I won't. You will do it, or you won't eat, and you'll swim in your own waste. That choice is yours. You forget I don't care about you. I am the emperor; YOU are nothing."

The governor sat down, leaning against the bars. He was colder, hungrier, and thirstier than he had ever been. His clothes were filthy, but he was not going to be bossed around. He would not do what the voice wanted.

The speaker started again, "Today, we're going to hear some tragic stories. We're going to hear people's experiences with the criminal justice system, or, as they call it, the injustice system. We're going to talk to a man who was accused of a crime, arrested, assumed guilty, and held without bail in jail for eight months. During that time, the prosecutor had evidence in her possession that would exonerate him, but she refused to look at it. There was nothing his defense attorney could do. We'll also hear from a researcher about how financial ability affects outcomes throughout the criminal case process. His findings show that those without financial means are at a significant disadvantage throughout the entire criminal charging and conviction process at a higher rate than those with the financial ability to defend themselves using highly compensated attorneys and expert witnesses, regardless of race or ethnicity.

"We'll also discuss the multiple levels of justice and injustice within our system. If you would like to call into the show today, our number is 555—OUR—TURN."

Instead of fighting to ignore the speaker and their guests, the governor now found it simpler to just listen. At least he did not feel as alone, and the people hosting and telling their stories made him feel somewhat connected to the world outside his cage.

Time passed, and with no outside light, he could not tell what time of day or night it was or how long it had been since he had woken up in the cage. It felt like a long time, days at least, maybe a week or more. He had no idea. He finally dozed off. When he woke up, the lighting in the cage had changed. He looked around and noticed that one of the lights on one of the small lanterns had gone out. Either someone had turned it off, or the battery had died. Whatever the reason, it was not comforting. It was a change for the worse. That was not a good thing. If it was simply a dead battery, he was sure he would not be able to afford what the voice would charge him for a new one. If the light went out or was gone because someone decided it should go, that was not good in a more ominous way. If the lights went out one at a time, he would eventually be in total darkness, in a cage, in only God knows where.

The hunger and the cold ate at him. He looked to where the cloth had been placed and stared at it. He did not want to capitulate, but he was not interested in a hunger strike either. He was already starving. *The voice has been very clear about how it feels about my well-being.* With slow movement, he moved across the cage and stood over the cloth. For a long time, he simply stood and looked down at it. He then looked around at the cage sides and the bars that stood guard over the top of him. After a few more moments of arguing with himself, he bent over, picked the cloth up, and moved to the corner by the sliding door. He began to rub the first vertical bar to his right. Then he repeated these motions on the next one on his right, and then next, and the next…

When he finished cleaning every bar in the cage, he went back to the corner he had become accustomed to and sat down. After what seemed like a short time, the voice said, "I see you decided to do as you were told. That was smart. I will not need to fine you for non-compliance again. Of course, I will have to charge you a late fee. You're still going deeper into debt, but it won't cost you as much as it would have had you forced me to fine you again on top of the late fee. The next fine is going to be even more expensive, the same as it is for people who violated your rules on the outside. Your fines will keep getting bigger and accumulating, just like they do for folks that you fine. A warning: be careful not to continue to antagonize me. I welcome nothing more than to keep treating you like you have treated your subjects."

The governor snapped back, "You're an asshole. We must have rules for society to function; if people don't follow the rules, there must be a penalty."

"I must obviously agree, or I wouldn't be fining you," said the voice. "But I will tell you, I believe there can be other ways than making people dig bigger financial holes for themselves than those they couldn't afford to be in, to begin with."

"I'm so tired of listening to you and being lectured by you," the governor said, shaking his head and walking around his cage. "You've never had the responsibilities I have. You deal in small things, the little pictures. It's my job to look at the big things, the big picture. Fines and fees are simply ways to make sure things get done. They're just tools to ensure compliance. Those aren't things I need to deal with; they're just part of the processes that have worked for years."

"Who the hell are YOU to be lecturing me?" continued the governor. "I've been very successful in my life. I've been a well-respected governor. What the hell have you done? What gives you the right to be giving me lessons in governance?"

"I am nobody," said the voice. "But I am the voice of everyone who would say they disagree that you've done well for yourself. Those same people would also disagree that you're well-respected. You're respected by your followers, but there's no respect for you from those to whom you've shown no respect."

"Well, screw you and all of them right along with you," roared the governor. "I don't need or want their respect; I don't need to have them on my side to do the things I see that need to be done."

The voice replied, "I will say it again because you obviously haven't been paying attention. Here you are! Here with me, not out ruling over your domain. It looks to me like you may need a few more friends than what you think you have. Otherwise, you wouldn't be here.

"Back to the business at hand," said the voice. "You asked me a question before I left the last time. You asked me what we're going to do with you. The answer is that I'm not sure yet; we are still discussing that subject. All options are still on the table. We have our collective objectives, but we're still discussing whether our methods will help us meet those objectives. So far, the jury is still out. Until that is determined, I'm still YOUR emperor. Unlike you, I have a diverse group of opinions among my counselors. I'm YOUR EMPEROR because that's the way you treat people like me. But I'm THEIR LEADER. We're aligned on our objectives but still working out the details among our various factions about how to achieve them. When we have accomplished that, the answer to your question will be evident. In the meantime, what would you like to buy with your money?" asked the voice. "You must be very hungry."

"Before I ask what my choices are," said the governor, "will you answer me one more question?"

"It depends," the voice said.

"Depends on what?" the governor asked.

The voice answered, "It depends on the quality and thoughtfulness of your question."

"My question is, are you telling me that your group has an objective, and to reach that objective, it involved kidnapping me and holding me prisoner and that you are still debating what to do with me?"

The voice said, "You HAVE been paying attention; YES, we HAVE objectives; making you a guest or 'disappeared person' was not the objective. Yes, there are some who want you punished, to suffer the ways that they have suffered under you. The ones who have lost loved ones. Those who have had their lives shattered by your policies. Those who see their kids, their jobs, their livelihoods, and their homes at risk under your reign. There are several paths that have been discussed for you. You are correct in your thinking that you should be taking your situation seriously and personally. But, in this case, it's not all about you. However, the way we see it is that you may be instrumental in possible solutions. In that regard, what is done with you matters to them only as far as your usefulness. You always have thought too highly of yourself. In our reality, as we see it, you are just a part of a process. An instrumental part, we think, therefore, your future depends on how well we believe our strategy will positively affect our objectives."

The governor insisted, "You've not asked me for anything or told me what it is you want from me."

The voice answered him, "You're slow to understand things you do not like or agree with, but we believe that you're smart enough."

"Smart enough to do what?" asked the governor.

"I'm afraid that depends on you," replied the voice. "Your understanding and internalization of your experience here will determine what your future holds. It will determine if you even have a future, either here or away from here.

"Now," said the voice, "what would you like to buy on credit?"

"What are my choices?" asked the governor.

"You only have one choice. It's a combo special. A few slices of apple and a cup of juice for $10. Take it or leave it. Just think, if you didn't have to pay all those taxes and fees, you would have had enough money to buy some more food. In your obstinance, you got yourself fined for not obeying me. Think about what you do to the people that YOU rule over. You bleed them dry through taxes, fines, and fees and think you are doing them a favor for their own good."

"Is that the plan?" the governor asked. "To slowly starve me to death and then take me out in the woods somewhere and leave me to rot until someone finds my body?"

"You'll just have to wait and see what happens," the voice answered. "But think about what you just said."

The governor was silent as he fought the fogginess of his brain.

The sound of the voice broke into his thoughts, "You don't get it, do you? Can't you see how some citizens in your state might think the same way about you?"

"What do you mean?" said the governor.

"You are, figurately in most cases but literally in others, doing just that to the citizens of your state," said the voice. "Some of them are barely able to survive. Others are seeing all that they have worked for being taken away from them and given to someone else who you think deserves it more."

"But YOU don't understand," said the governor.

"Explain it to me," said the voice.

The governor replied, "We have a lot of people in this state with money, more than they need to live, while others are in poverty. Obviously, you don't care about those people, but I DO! Those people need help. We can't just let them continue to suffer. We NEED to level the standard of living more equitably to make things fairer. Most of those people, the ones who are well off, are not going to miss a few thousand dollars a year, and we can use that money to help those who are struggling."

The voice said, "Do you really believe that an average person, an average family, is not going to miss a few thousand dollars a year from their income? That is craziness, Governor! Even if they could live without that money for one year, it wouldn't be sustainable. Everyone knows that you will just take more. You just keep scraping away at what they have. What results have you gotten for that?"

"We've helped a lot of people with that money," said the governor.

"A lot of people would argue that you haven't," the voice cut in. "You have more homeless. You have made the streets of our cities open drug areas. Normal citizens are afraid to go into your major cities or walk down their streets. Stores are boarded up. Stores that ARE open have locked doors. Customers must ring a bell, or knock, and be checked out to see if they look like they are going to rob the place before they can even get in the store or shop."

"We're working on that!" said the governor. "We've requested more funds to help fight this problem."

"EXACTLY!!" said the voice. "You always need more money, but you don't solve the problems. You don't force the homeless that are drug addicted to get help," said the voice. "You even give them free drugs and make them off limits to any enforcement actions. Take those people out of the equation, then put focus on the mentally ill and the truly homeless."

"You may not know this, but those two problems are usually combined," retorted the governor.

"I do know that," said the voice, "but you ignore both. You cannot deal with either one until you get the drug issue out of the way. Then, you can focus on the mental health issue. There are places that have successfully dealt with these problems, but you don't like their solutions. Your logic astounds me. You let them live and behave like animals under the banner of not offending their 'rights.' Your state has some of the most stringent and expensive septic and sewer regulations in the country, but you let people defecate and urinate on public streets and on other people's property without issue. Human waste management is either an issue or it isn't. Why are you letting that go on? The rest of the citizens, the ones who live by your rules and laws, must walk, drive, work, and live around those people violating your laws and simple common decency, and they are treated as though their 'rights' don't matter. If you cleaned up the drug and mental health issues, you could help the ones who truly are homeless because of economics, joblessness, and affordability. Those who cannot afford a place to live. You know, some of the ones who may have been made homeless by your policies and everything you people do that makes the cost of simply living increase! Governor, there are roughly 700,000 homeless people in this country. You and your like-minded politicians have made no discernible impact on the problem and, in fact, have made it worse. On the other hand, you have welcomed between ten and twenty million and counting illegals into this country and provided them with health care, housing, phones, and income. For a fraction of the money you spent on them, you could have addressed the homeless, drug, and mental health issues of our own citizens and provided them all with a job instead of handouts and enabling. It appears that most, but not all, of the homeless are US citizens, and several are veterans. Shame on you, Governor. Shame be on you!"

"We ARE working on those issues! We've spent millions on these problems," said the governor.

"Yes, you have, but your results are a miserable failure. For all the millions of dollars that you spend, you cannot prove that you've made a positive difference. It's time to try some other approaches. Seriously, work the problems," said the voice, "and you may even have more support for helping the ones who have truly been made homeless through poverty."

"Like what?" said the governor.

"Like quit treating everyone with a problem as a victim," snapped the voice. "Some of their problems are self-inflicted. Stop paying people not to work or giving money to illegals who have never paid a dime in taxes. Your own citizens are in trouble and cannot get that kind of help. You just keep making things worse. You talk about affordable housing, but all your regulations keep increasing the costs of housing. You heard some of their stories on the programs I've been playing for you. Homes are out of the financial reach for lower-paid working people. If they are in housing of their own, and they fall behind in payment, the fees and penalties that get levied on them make it impossible to keep up or dig their way out of the hole you put them in. And to add insult to injury, you allow big companies to buy up single-dwelling homes just to rent them back to those who could have been potential homeowners. The big companies rent those homes at an inflated rent price higher than the cost of ownership would have been. Why are you allowing that? Governor, the way you like to tax things, why haven't you placed a heavy tax on each of those homes being bought by those companies that are buying up those single-dwelling homes? Individuals are being outbid by those companies, and those companies are driving the prices up. How is letting them do that helping the aspiring homeowner? Taxing each one of those homes that those companies buy would be the best tax application you could do. You could make the business of buying up single-dwelling homes and renting them back at an increased rate an unprofitable business. They would be one of the few businesses that could not pass that tax on to the renters because they would not be able to afford the rent. Driving those companies out of the housing market would bring the costs of housing back down and be of help to potential homebuyers. Your tax gains from that action would be significant—short-lived, but significant—and you would have done the country a service.

"Governor, you are a big part of your own problems. You keep raising the cost of gas. The highest tax in the nation, with no visible reason other than to try to force people to drive less or force people who can't afford your inflated gas prices in the first place to buy an expensive electric vehicle. How are working people or people on fixed incomes supposed to suck that up? When those same people cannot afford the highway and bridge tolls that you charge, you fine them for not being able to pay, and the fines and penalties keep growing. Once again, you just keep burying them deeper. If they still cannot pay the tolls and the fines, you suspend their driver's license. How are they supposed to get to work?"

"We have a big job," said the governor, trying to address all these problems. "WE are making progress. We've spent more money on these problems than any other administration in our state's history."

"Governor, drop your campaign speeches with me. Your policies are not working. Yes, you have had some small successes, but at what costs?" replied the voice. "You spend a lot of money and want to spend even more, but nothing is getting better. Things are getting worse. You must at least see that I'm telling you the truth about what's happening. It's too bad you couldn't do what wise emperors did in ancient times."

"What did they do?" asked the governor.

"They took a break from listening to their advisers and nobles, all of whom had a vested and financial interest in the rulers' decisions," the voice explained. "They disguised themselves and went out among the people to learn for themselves what was really happening in their realms. Maybe in today's world, that wasn't possible for you, given your visibility, but you could have found other ways to hear the people's voices. When you do listen, you only listen to the high-profile victims, the people who are continually victims. You don't listen to the others, the ones YOU are victimizing. That's why we've been providing you the opportunity to hear people's stories during the programs we've provided for your listening pleasure."

"I think I've heard enough of that propaganda; I know what you're doing. How about just turning it off?"

"What are we doing, Governor?"

"You're using sob stories to try and soften me up," answered the governor.

"To what end?" asked the voice.

"So maybe I'd look at some other points of view?"

"But, Governor, your answer assumes that you will have the opportunity to make use of those new insights."

"What do you mean by that?" asked the governor.

"Maybe we just like the satisfaction of knowing that you were at least exposed to some different perspectives. If that has all been for naught, that would be disappointing."

"Disappointing for who? The governor asked.

"Oh, you most of all, by all means; it will be you who will most regret not opening your mind to some other perspectives," answered the voice.

"That sounds like a threat," said the governor.

The voice laughed and said, "I have no need to threaten. I answered your question."

The governor stood quiet for a few minutes, looked at the direction of the voice, and said, "I hope you know that we've been doing what we believe is best for our citizens, for the state, and for the planet. Do you really believe we are that far off track? We have a lot of support for what we're doing."

"I believe you believe that to be true," said the voice, "but you're living in your own heads. You're spinning your own narratives. In a very crude analogy, you folks are drinking your own bath water. The path you are on isn't going to get you what you think it will. You are dismantling the policies and institutions that worked and replacing them with non-solutions based upon repeatedly failed ideologies. Governor, you have people leaving your state in droves. Yes, I know you have other people coming in from other states. But look where they are coming from. They're coming from states whose self-destructive timetable has moved faster than yours. Although I must say, you have done your best to catch up."

"I disagree," said the governor. "We still have a lot of people who support our way of thinking and doing—people who support the taxes and the redistribution of wealth that's so necessary for making the kind of social progress we've neglected for so long."

"That is true," said the voice. "Look at it this way: you have no-income and low-income citizens who are very poor, who maybe work or do not work. They receive more from society than they can contribute financially. Most people understand that and have no problem helping those who cannot help themselves. Then you have a second group, the middle-income earners, who are the largest population of what we see as three groups, at least for now. The middle-income earners are shrinking rapidly. The people in this category have a range of incomes. They're not rich but are perhaps comfortable. Some of them live paycheck to paycheck but pay their own way. A sizable portion of this middle group has had what you call disposable income, money available after paying the bills. With your taxes and inflation, that money is quickly slipping away from them. The people in this middle group are the ones you are hitting the hardest. The ones who have worked, saved, and done all the things that the old society said they should do to be successful. This group is working hard to make a living, support their families, and hopefully retire at the end of their working lives. Now, you're taking all of that away from them and redistributing THEIR money to fund YOUR initiatives. Your goal appears to be to achieve EQUALITY, NOT EQUITY. Equity considers the amount or quality of inputs and the resultant outputs of those inputs. Equality means everybody is entitled to the same outcome regardless of individual input, talent, energy, intellect, or effort. You want everyone to have equal outcomes!"

"But—said the governor, interrupting the voice.

The voice continued speaking, talking over the governor. "Then, Governor, you have the high-income earners. They have more discretionary money, so your incremental and multiple tax increases don't affect them the way those increases affect the middle earners. The increased cost of gas, food, and housing does not hurt the high earners. They can absorb the added costs. They don't normally have a problem of being charged late fees that get compounded or added onto. If they are in court, it's usually by choice. This group has very little interaction with criminal courts; if they do, they'll usually have the prosecutor on their side at no cost to them. This group doesn't much care about what happens to 'criminals.' Unless they themselves have been the victims of crime.

"If the wealthy do get into a problem, legal or otherwise, they have the money to hire professionals to deal with it. Everything is fine with them. Any problem they can write a check to solve is not a problem. They can virtue signal by supporting your causes and feel good about themselves. They get to tell people how open-minded they are. They may have a little less discretionary money under your rule, but so far, they've had no real skin in the game. So far, Governor, they can afford you.

"However, Governor, once your redistribution policies destroy the middle class, that only leaves the upper-income earners to fund your programs and pay your taxes. JUST imagine what will happen when you come for a more significant portion of THEIR money to make up for all the lost tax revenues from the unemployed and laid-off workers, from closed businesses, and the new larger homeless population you're going to create. As Margaret Thatcher, the famous past prime minister of the UK, famously said, 'The problem with socialism is that, sooner or later, you are going to run out of other people's money.' The remaining group of high earners will have the money to fight you. I don't think they're really paying attention now. They are too busy feeling superior and good about themselves and their progressiveness that they do not see your hand going even deeper into their pockets. Those that have been paying attention have already begun to leave your state before you start to drain them, too."

The governor smiled and said, "There is one thing you're missing from your little scenario there. We've already thought about what you say is happening and will continue to happen. We're smarter than you think we are. We have OUR objectives too. We know where the breaking point is for most of that middle group you speak of. We do not intend to 'drain them' to use your term, at least not completely. That would be counterproductive to our objective. We just intend to equalize the standard of living among the middle and lower groups. And yes, we can then work to reduce the amount of discretionary income of that higher-earning group, as you call it, for a more equitable distribution of resources and lifestyles. So, yes, you're correct about the long term and our objectives. At a point, after we have equalized the lower groups, we'll also need to equalize the two remaining groups: the lower and the existing upper group. When we're done, we'll simply have one remaining group: a single middle group."

The voice said, "If I'm hearing you correctly, that doesn't seem like you think it's going to be a big problem for you."

"No, we don't think it will be," said the governor. "Even if I'm gone, it's almost too late for them to fight what we've put in place effectively. The laws that we've put into effect are foundational to OUR objectives. Even if the remaining wealthy, upper earners as you call them, do leave the state, we've placed new taxes on the selling of their homes and businesses. We're putting environmental regulations on their existing homes that must be met, at considerable expense, before they can sell them. Those actions will make it more expensive to sell a home or a business and try to leave the state. Maybe we won't get everything we want from them, but we'll get plenty. We have enough people in the right places to make it happen. As you pointed out earlier, we have enough voter provisions in place to keep our side winning elections and our people in office for the foreseeable future. So, even if you kill me, it will not make a difference to the outcomes we intend."

"Governor," said the voice, "I'm surprised you openly admit that's your real plan," the voice said.

"Do you remember the famous quote about transparency and the stupidity of the voters??" asked the governor.

"Refresh my memory," the voice said.

The governor continued, "It was a comment made by the infamous consultant on Obamacare. His statement got a lot of coverage in the conservative press. He said, 'Lack of transparency is a huge political advantage. Basically, call it the stupidity of the voter, or whatever, but basically, that was really critical to getting Obamacare to pass.' Nothing has changed," said the governor. "Both lack of transparency and the stupidity of the voters are still our most useful weapons."

"Thank you for refreshing my memory, Governor. I do remember him and his quote. That information came out after the passing of the legislation, didn't it?"

"Yes, it did," said the governor.

"What do you think would happen if your words about the plan you just talked about were made public now?" asked the voice.

"Probably nothing; I guess there would be a little flap about it from the conservative press. It would get some airtime on the conservative stations, the few of them that exist. Our supporters have been trained not to listen to anything those stations say, so it won't matter. Also, don't forget how good we are at working on the narratives. Not much harm would be done to our agenda. As one of our people was recorded saying on a hot mic, 'We just lie about it and blame the other side.' We'll distribute our talking points to our supportive media, and the issue will blow over and be forgotten. Again, nobody pays much attention to what we, the government, are really doing anyway."

"Governor, you and I may very well get a chance to test your theory about how much damage your own words would do to your agenda and your party if released to the public right before the next election."

"What do you mean?" asked the governor.

Brushing the governor's question aside, the voice challenged the governor. "I thought surely by now that you would have come around to thinking about real fixes to some of the problems of the state's people. Fixes that could raise people up instead of taking more down. Maybe be more focused on specific problems that could be addressed for a lot less money. There are a lot of things that need to be done to truly reduce poverty instead of increasing it while serving the needs of the state at the same time."

"What are you talking about?" asked the governor.

The voice answered, "Maybe to start with, again, do not assume everyone is a victim, and stop creating victims where they shouldn't exist. I think most people understand there are people who cannot work, people who are disabled in one form or another, or in other debilitating circumstances. Those people are not an issue. But for others, maybe create training and work programs. How about creating guaranteed jobs to go along with the guaranteed payments you want to hand out? There are multiple ways to do that. There are thousands of ways the state could put people to work doing things that need to be done and, at the same time, begin reversing the entitlement and dependency models you've created. You'd still be spending money but getting results for the money spent.

"You could also do a lot of work on alternatives to fines, penalties, and punishments on the people who can least afford them. More pointed interventions, instead of broad brushing every problem with the same brush, raising taxes and throwing money at it."

"What do you mean by that?" asked the governor.

"Maybe you could have 'scholarship' bridge or road tolls for working people who meet family, financial, or healthcare-specific criteria. Again, don't just assume you have to raise the tolls for everyone to cover the extra costs. You will just exacerbate existing problems by doing that. Get creative; maybe you could spread the toll-financing payment over a longer period. Or maybe give low-wage earners a lower standard monthly or weekly rate based on income or other selected criteria. Maybe instead of raising the minimum wage for everyone, you could have targeted the need."

"What do you mean?" asked the governor.

The voice explained, "Does a kid making minimum wage and living with their parents have the same bills and needs as the same wage earner who lives alone or the sole wage earner for a family? Of course not! By broad brushing it and giving the minimum wage to everyone, the costs rise for everyone who uses those services. Even the ones making the new minimum wage. Think of someone on a fixed income; by raising the minimum wage across the board, you just took money away from them to give it to the kid living with their parents. Why do that? One study reported that only one-third of the people receiving minimum wage were single earners living alone. The others were either living with their parents, married, or living with a person of sustainably higher income. Maybe these are not good ideas, but they are thoughts that are alternative to just spending the people's money and harming many of them while trying to help others."

The governor said, "But if you did that with minimum wage, you'd have two people doing the same job and making different pay. Is that fair?"

"Maybe not, but with your minimum wage, they now make almost as much money as entry-level professionals with college degrees, tradespeople, or other professionals. Those people are doing a higher level of work than the fast-food employees and making basically the same amount? How is that fair?" asked the voice. "With your minimum wage increases, you are putting people out of work because businesses cannot afford them and will ultimately automate those jobs. What are you going to do with those people who are now unemployed and may not yet have the skills for a higher-level job? Raise more taxes to pay them not to work? Fast-food jobs used to be viewed as a way of training the nation's work-force. They were considered introductory jobs, jobs that provided training and the discipline of working. For years, they were only intended to be stepping stones into higher-level and higher-paying jobs. They have now also become ways for seniors to supplement their fixed incomes. Your policies have changed all that, and not for the good that you think it has been. I'm sure, Governor, that raising the minimum wage was a good 'sound bite' and 'feel good' fix, and that got you a lot of votes from those who benefited from it while their jobs lasted. My point is and continues to be that problems need to be analyzed, and the implications of various possible solutions need to be studied for their impact, intended and unintended. Come up with laser-focused solutions that specifically address the problems you were trying to fix instead of making it worse or causing collateral problems in other parts of the system.

"Speaking of that," said the voice, "college and university tuitions are out of control. You love to set targets for industry and private enterprise to meet; what is stopping you from attacking college and university costs in the same way?"

"We're addressing that," said the governor.

"How?" said the voice.

"Well, for one," said the governor, "we are creating a fund for every child who meets our criteria to use when they reach adulthood. These funds can be used to make a down payment on a house or pay for their education; it will be their choice. We're also creating pathways to higher education through scholarships for minorities and others who've been the least capable of securing an education. We've supported the federal government's forgiveness of student loans. We are doing great work in that area," bragged the governor.

"Again, you're using tax money that you'll have to raise to pay for those programs and will require additional tax raises to continue funding them," said the voice. "It's always tax and spend with you. If you have a surplus, you must spend it. Even when you have a surplus, you keep asking for more taxes so you can spend that too."

"We're doing the best we can to address all the inequities that exist in our state. It takes money to do that," insisted the governor.

The voice shot back, "That's the problem! You never look for ways to REDUCE spending! Since that concept is apparently alien to you, let me give you some ideas. Why don't you dictate to the colleges and universities that they set budget and tuition 'REDUCTION TARGETS' like you do for other industries? After all, they are STATE institutions. Every school that offers an undergraduate or master's in business administration degree should be given cost-reduction targets and tuition-cost reduction targets to be met in the same time periods that you give auto manufacturers.

Let's say you start with a target of a 30 percent reduction in costs and tuition within five years. Then, keep the pressure on, with ongoing targets, until we have gotten rid of the fluff and other waste out of the educational system and made higher education affordable again. Less indoctrination and more education. If those schools cannot figure out how to reduce those costs or meet the tuition targets, their accreditations should be canceled in those business-related disciplines. Those schools should not be allowed to offer a course in business management if they cannot manage themselves the way almost all other businesses are expected to. Why should anyone hire graduates from those schools if they, themselves, cannot successfully manage their own affairs? Governor, you could put the business schools in these colleges to work to help solve the problem they have created. As you like to say, sacrifices must be made. Why not let these overpriced and vainglorious schools sacrifice along with the rest of us."

"But those are just students," said the governor. "They're not ready to do that level of work."

"I think you underestimate them," said the voice. "They have professors who are making a lot of money for doing little to promote the welfare of this country. You have master's-level students who need real-world problems to work on. Put those professors to work with their students to figure it out. If they cannot figure it out, then the professors are incompetent. Students should not get a degree in the discipline of a professor who can only profess, but not do."

The governor thought for a minute and then said, "That's totally unrealistic. We could never make that happen."

"You think that way, so it is that way!" said the voice. "Change your way of thinking. A tremendous amount of money from your state budget goes to those institutions. A great deal of money from the state lottery goes into those institutions. Yeah, I know you sold the lottery as supporting K–12, but only a small percentage in comparison goes to K–12. Only when the state got caught in that lie did you start providing money to K–12. Most of what's left of lottery money after paying the winners and paying the expenses of running the program in your state goes to higher education in one form or another. If the costs and tuition are reduced, maybe you wouldn't need to use taxes or to keep raising taxes to pay for college scholarships. You could have looked at the numbers and made something work or at least made a dent in the problem. Force the schools to come up with less expensive solutions. Make them part of the solution, not just the problem. Work to eliminate the need for student loans in the first place. Make that a target. Why just keep increasing the costs of college and then expect people who cannot afford to pay for college themselves or for their own kids to have to pay even higher taxes to send someone else's kids to college? That makes no sense!"

"What you're saying sounds good, but it would be hard to implement," said the governor. "The way we're doing it is fairer and simpler. Much fairer than what you propose. We can spread the cost of going to college out over a lot more people so that it's not a burden for anyone and helps these young people to start their life without being in debt."

"You're not listening. IT IS costing people who currently cannot afford your taxes and fees in the first place. Maybe they cannot afford to send their own kids to college or have already paid for their own college. Then you believe it's a great idea to tax those same people to send someone else or someone else's kids to go to college. It is that middle group that you have lost. The ones you are continuing to beat down with your taxes. If you attack the problem of the costs and the tuition at its source, you solve multiple problems at once."

"Just so you know," said the governor, "I'm listening to what you say. I can't say I agree with any of it, but you've raised some things for consideration. If I wasn't here in this cold cage, only God knows where I might put my advisers to work on these ideas. But here I am. It's too bad you didn't try to approach me when I was free to implement your ideas."

"Governor," said the voice, "people have talked to you and your administration about all these things. NONE of you have listened. You missed your chance, and now you're paying the price for yourself and for those others who didn't listen."

The governor looked at the floor thoughtfully for a moment and then said, "I'm hungry and thirsty. I think I've had all the lectures I can stand for now. I'd like to get some food."

"Of course," said the voice. "If you remember, I came to you to discuss your food situation. It was you who started the 'lecture' with your questions. Now, it's your choice: take the combo or leave it. We're offering you a glimpse of what it's like to be one of your subjects, Your Majesty."

The governor said, "I'll take apple slices and the juice."

The food appeared at the slot. The governor heard footsteps walking away.

After picking up the food, the governor moved to his spot on the floor against the bars and started to pick up an apple slice.

The flickering light reflecting on the plastic drapes of his cage caught the governor's attention. At first, it looked like a colorful swirling cloud. He watched it change shape and come into a blurry focus.

He moved closer to it and then realized he needed to step back from it to determine better what was coming into view. The drape material made the images distorted, but as he stood watching it, he could make out what looked like lockers, like those in a gym or fitness center. The camera moved, and he could see what looked like a large woman from the back. She had long dark hair in a ponytail down to the base of her neck. She was wearing a knee-length, multicolored floral dress.

The governor looked around to see if anyone else was watching this scene with him. His eyes focused on the screen, and he called out to the voice, "Are you here?" but there was no answer. He was alone except for the image unfolding in front of him. As he watched, from the position and movement of her arms, it looked like the woman with her back to him was unbuttoning the front of her dress.

As she slowly turned, she appeared sideways to the camera and was looking directly across the locker room. Her face and full black beard came into view as she turned her head and looked directly at the camera for just a moment. "What the..." escaped from the governor's mouth.

They turned their face to look back across the locker room. As they continued to unbutton the dress down its front with one hand, they slipped the other hand inside the dress below its waist. The governor could see movement inside the dress but was not sure what was causing it.

When they undid the last button at the bottom of the dress, they raised both arms and, taking a shoulder of the dress in each hand, peeled the dress from their shoulders. As the dress moved down off the shoulders, a hairy chest and large belly came into view. The person in the image let go of the dress, and it fell to the floor. The governor stepped back in horror as he saw the profile of the huge erection protruding out from under the belly from what, for all purposes, was a man ready to have sex.

The governor looked around again, hoping to see or hear something that told him he was not alone. That someone could explain to him what he was seeing and why he was seeing it. "What is this?" he yelled. "Why are you showing this to me? This is disgusting, you pervert!"

There was no answer.

He looked back at the images on the screen as the camera started a slow scan across the room. Moving from the man with the erection, past a series of lockers, to a young woman with her back to the camera. She was undressing for the shower in the background and was down to her panties. It appeared to the governor that she heard something behind her that caused her to turn around. As she turned, the governor froze where he stood and screamed, "NOOOOOOOO! You son of a bitch; don't do this. I'll kill you!"

As the young woman turned toward the man, she too screamed and started backing up, trying to cover herself with pieces of her clothing that she had laid on the bench beside her. Her retreat was stopped by the lockers behind her. As she dropped to the floor with one arm outstretched, trying to stop the attacker's advance with the other hand clutching her clothes to her, trying to hide her nakedness, the look of horror on her face was matched only by that of her father, the governor, as he too dropped to his knees crying out loud. Putting his hands first over his ears to drown out her screams and then over his eyes to stop the visions scorching his brain. In his hysterics, he did not realize that the images had disappeared.

He stayed on his knees until, exhausted, he finally collapsed prone on the floor, continuing to sob. The next sound he heard, other than his own, was the voice, "Having a hard day, are we, Governor?"

The governor rose and ran toward the sound of the voice. "You! You better hope I don't get out of here. I'll have you hunted down. I'll kill you myself, and it will be a painful death. How could you do that to her? That's my daughter."

"Be careful what you say, Governor; that sounds like hate speech to me. I might have to call your new hotline and report you; there are significant fines for that type of behavior, even jail time.

"Tell me, Governor, how should I react to what you just saw happen? Should I feel the sadness and outrage you're feeling right now, like other fathers who have had this happen? Or should I take your approach that this is just the price of the transition to the new world of the rights of gender expression? I could be mistaken by your behavior, but I don't think you are as appreciative of that person's expression of gender as you have been in the speeches you've given. I specifically don't recall seeing any press releases or hearing about any press conferences from you condemning these attacks when the same thing happened to someone else's daughter. They're just infrequent occurrences on our path to enlightenment and inclusivity, RIGHT? Everyone must make sacrifices for the new order; isn't that what you say?" said the voice. "I guess your daughter just turned out to be one of those sacrifices."

"YOU did this!" the governor yelled as he shook the bars of his cage. "YOU! YOU DID THIS, and you will pay. Those cases are very rare, and you know it, you asshole. You had to have something to do with it."

"NO, Governor, I did NOT do it. YOU DID IT. You, your friends, and your supporters. Welcome to the other side. The side of living with YOUR beliefs. When your friends tell you that what happened to your daughter was an isolated case, will that make you feel better about what happened in that locker room?"

The governor raged at the voice, shook the bars, and looked for something to throw, something to hit, but he had nothing. He was powerless and impotent against all that was happening to him, and he felt anger down to the core of his being.

When he had spent his fury at the bars of the cage and quieted himself, he returned to the food and started to eat when the plastic drapes again started to come to life. The governor uncoiled from the floor as fast as his stiff, cold body could move. A sense of dread swept over him as he had just been hit by a heart-stopping blast of cold water from a fire hose. Unsteady on his feet, he hesitated, not knowing whether to move toward the colors on the drape or get as far away from it as he could in the limited space available.

He chose the latter and moved to the far side of the cage, steadying himself with his back against the bars. Again, there was no intro-duction, just the area on the drape coming to life. As it came into focus, he could see it was a cityscape. Within moments, he was able to recognize iconic images of a downtown area of the state's most populous city.

It appeared to be near nightfall. The governor was familiar with the area shown, a small park surrounded by businesses and restau-rants. As he watched, he thought about what the voice had said about the crime, the homelessness, and the drugs. The area was now devoid of the tourists and locals, along with their families, who used to fill the benches with blankets spread on the ground to enjoy the beauty of the park and the sense of community. It was no longer a safe place to be for them.

Instead, what remained, and what now populated the image on the screen, were the homeless, the city zombies, the drugged-out remains of what once was a person, even possibly a contributing member of society until the rulers of the new order, like himself, had determined that life and society were being too hard on them and they must have their freedom to self-destruct and take cities down with them. Of course, there are also the true homeless, those who perhaps had lost their job or been replaced by automation, those who could no longer afford the high home or apartment prices, and the increased cost of groceries.

While the governor was lost in thought, the camera moved to a smaller area of the park and focused on a bench where two men sat. It was an odd pairing. One of the men, skinny with scraggy hair, a filthy beard, and worn-out clothes, was folding up a paper envelope and putting it into his pocket.

The trim young man beside him, looking out of place in this setting in his clean, stylish clothes, was beginning to nod his head forward and then throw his head back before nodding forward again with his chin on his chest. The young man tried to stand but immediately sat back down and tried to remain upright on the bench. His movements were erratic, as his body appeared to spasm in disjointed movement.

As the camera lens zoomed in, the other man got up and moved out of camera range, leaving the young man on the bench. By the time the camera was close to him, he had lost consciousness. He was lying on his back with one leg against the back of the bench and the other hanging off the front, touching the ground.

As the camera came in closer to the young man on the bench, he turned his head toward the camera and began to vomit. The governor screamed out to the room beyond his cage in pain and panic, "OH NO, not HIM too; YOU are so dead; if my son dies, I will find you. If it's the last thing I ever do, I'll get you for what you've done to my family. My poor children, my wife? How can you do this?"

Once again, there was no answer to his words, only the silence of a broken, crying man lying in a heap on a cold, hard floor.

At the sound of the voice's footsteps, the governor's body revolted and moved up against the steadying presence of the bars at his back.

"I see this has been another difficult viewing for you," said the voice.

The governor, for one of the few times in his life, was at a loss for words. He sat on the floor, his head involuntarily moving back and forth, trying to force his mind to push the images out. All he could do was feel: feel hatred for the voice, feel hatred for those who could do such horrible things to his children. They had done nothing wrong. They were good, decent kids. They had a great future ahead of them.

Overwhelmed with emotion, unable to gather the strength to stand up, he simply rolled his head back against the bars behind him for support, drew in a deep breath, and just stared in the direction of the voice. The voice said, "What? Aren't you going to blame me for this too?"

The governor continued to stare into the emptiness of his cage without a word.

"It's a shame what's going on in the world, don't you think?" asked the voice.

Tears appeared in the governor's eyes and made their way slowly down his cheeks, but still, he remained silent.

The voice said, "I want you to think about something. Last year, 112,000 people in this country died just from fentanyl alone, over 1,500 in one county of your state. Think of all those parents, the spouses, the children, going through the agony of losing a loved one like that. You and your friends not only allow it, but you also support it. Your friends in DC, with their open borders, promote it. Your friends in China make the drugs and support their distribution to and in this country while strictly prohibiting it in their own country.

"Governor, I'd think that would make you all feel like you're being used. Used by the cartels, the Chinese, and everyone else involved. But for some reason that I don't understand, you don't feel that way. Instead of having sympathy for you, I'm ashamed for you. You, among only a handful of people, could have done something about this problem.

"If you've lost a child to this problem, you just joined an ever-growing community of grieving parents. I guess some will have sympathy for you for losing a child, but as an enabler of these needless deaths, they probably won't feel sympathy for you or welcome you into their fold of loved ones of those lost to drug-related deaths. In fact, I'm quite sure some will think you got what you deserved."

The governor just sat and stared into the silence of the empty room.

When he came out of his shock and was able to move, the governor reached for the apple slices, mindful that the "meal" did not amount to much. He took small bites and chewed each, slowly relishing the taste. He finished the fruit and sipped at the grape-colored juice, wondering how he was going to survive what he was being put through. His mind went to his children and then to his wife. *She must be going through hell*, he thought. He wished he could be with her, to share their grief together, to support each other as they always had.

The speaker startled him from his thoughts. "Today, we'll share the story of a woman who commuted to her job in one of our major cities. You may have read it in the newspapers. She resigned from her job and took another one in a different city to escape her daily commuting nightmare. Her story is of the decay of a city that she once found beautiful and vibrant. Her daily walking commute was plagued by harassment from people out of their minds on drugs or some other malady. She was exposed to fentanyl on public transportation. Over a two-year period, the building in which she worked had been locked down twice because of active shooters outside. On two separate occasions not associated with the lockdowns, upon leaving work, she passed two different dead bodies lying in the street while police conducted their investigations. We'll talk about these and other experiences from others later in the program..."

The strain of his ordeal catching up with the governor, he felt the tiredness in his body. As he started to drift off, his last thoughts were that, with everything that had happened, he must reconcile himself to the reality that he may never see his children or his wife again. Then he slept.

# PART II

The governor woke up cold and groggy. He tried to sit up and felt the restraint across his chest holding him in place. His eyes open now; he realized that he was already sitting up. He quickly looked around and down at the seat belt holding him in place. He was in a car. He looked out the front window. The car was parked on the side of a road with a hill ahead enveloped by trees on each side. He could see nothing beyond the trees and the empty road in front of him. In the rear-facing mirrors, he could see the road behind him disappearing over a hill. He unbuckled the seat belt and turned to look in the back seat, expecting to see someone there. Again, nothing!

The governor pushed the start button on the dash and felt the relief of the dashboard lights greeting him. He realized as he looked at the screen that he was in an electric vehicle. The screen told him the percent remaining on the battery charge and that the mileage remaining was zero. At least the car had started. He put the vehicle in drive, and it started to move forward. He didn't know how far he could go, where he was, or where to go, but he was excited to be free. The car moved slowly, but it was moving. "Prompt" warnings appeared on the screen, informing him of the low battery. As he drove, he could feel the car slowing down; the hills were the hardest on the car, draining the battery further and causing it to slow even more. The warning signs on the screen became more insistent about getting off the road and recharging the battery. He didn't care. He would not stop. He needed to get somewhere, some place with another human and a phone.

As he started up another hill, the car came to a stop and put itself in park. *Now what?* he thought. He sat in the car and waited for another car to come along. After what felt like about an hour, without another vehicle passing him, he decided he would start walking. He needed to somehow connect with his wife and his children. The cold bit into him as he walked. Maybe he would have been smarter to stay in the car. Staying with the car is what the experts tell you anyway. His desire to put more distance between himself and those who had taken him forced him to keep moving. He felt safer being on the move, even as he was second-guessing himself on the advisability of leaving the car.

He had no idea how long or how far he had walked. The clouds obscured the sun, but it seemed like it had been quite a bit higher in the sky when he woke up in the car. He was exposed to the cold with only the clothes that he was wearing at the time of his capture. His food intake had been next to nothing, and his body ached. His legs were weak and unsteady with the exertion of walking up and down the hills. His lungs burned. He was exhausted. His body was demanding he stop, to rest. His mind was telling him that if he obeyed his body's command, he could die out here. He kept going.

He was not sure at first what he was hearing, but his ears were picking up some kind of sound that came and went beyond the silence of the woods, the wind, and an occasional bird or animal noise. It sounded like rushing water. Maybe it was a stream or a river. If that was the case, maybe he could follow it and find someone. That hopeful thought was immediately followed by the discouraging thought that maybe he would find out he had been walking upstream instead of downstream. Depending on where he was, the direction of the flowing water could be very important. He kept to his path in the middle of the narrow road. The noise alternated between sound and silence. If it was water, maybe the denser stands of trees or the hills in his path were periodically blocking the sound as he moved along the road.

He pressed on, hoping that whatever was causing the noise would be helpful. As he crested another small hill and rounded a slight bend in the road, he saw a building with lights. Beyond that, he saw the blur of a car or truck on another road passing by the building. He kept moving forward. As he got closer to the building and the end of the road he had been on, he passed a wooden barricade in the middle of the road. Once past the barricade, he turned to look at the sign attached. It was a highway department sign that said, "Road Closed." *That explains why no cars came my way while I was in the car*, he thought. As a second thought came to mind, a chill went through him. If the road was closed, why had he been left where he was? Was he not supposed to be found? Had he been left there to die? What if he had not decided to strike off on foot? As he turned back toward the building, the thoughts about the closed road and its implications left him. His focus became getting to that building, to warmth, to safety. As he got closer to the building, he saw gas pumps outside and a brightly lit "OPEN" sign in a window. The sign pulled him forward. He was almost running now. Wanting out of the cold, wanting something to eat and drink, and, most of all, to let someone know where he was so they could get him safely away from whatever this had been.

He opened the door and went inside. He did not see anyone. He called out, "Is anyone here?"

"Hold on," a voice came through a door behind the counter. "Yeah, what do you need?" said a large older man emerging through it.

"I need a phone! Do you have one?" said the governor.

"Yeah, I do; what do you need it for?" asked the man.

"I've been kidnapped. I need to call the police," the governor told him.

"I can do that for you. Where did you come from?" asked the man.

"Up the road, the car I was driving died and is still up there," said the governor.

"Do you need some gas?" the man behind the counter asked. "I could get you some and get you on your way to where..."

"You don't understand," interrupted the governor. "I was kidnapped! Gas isn't going to do any good. It's an electric car."

The man behind the counter laughed. "Well, no wonder you got kidnapped. Driving an electric car out here's pretty stupid. There are no chargers anywhere near here that I know of, and from what I hear, those cars don't take to the cold all that well. More people would be walking like you are if they owned one of those things up here."

"NO, damn it, I didn't get kidnapped from the car. I'm the governor! I've been kidnapped! I need to talk to the police," the governor barked, his irritation growing.

"Ok, ok, are we in any danger here, from your kidnappers, I mean?" asked the man.

"No, I don't think so anyway," answered the governor. "I haven't seen them today."

"Well, just in case," the worker said as he reached under the counter and brought out a rifle with a magazine protruding from the body of the gun.

"What are you going to do with that? Just call the police. I order you to," said the governor.

"First of all, there, Governor, I don't work for you. If you're the governor of the state, which I'm not even sure you are, I don't really like you, and I don't think I want to die if your friends come here looking for you before we can get the cops here. We're pretty far out up here. We're basically on our own for quite a while when trouble happens. So why don't you just calm down and maybe get away from any windows just in case your friends are looking for you."

"They're not my friends, damn it! They kidnapped me!" shouted the governor. "What kind of gun is that?" He pointed at the rifle on the countertop.

"It's an AR-15," explained the worker.

"It's an assault rifle then. An automatic rifle! I outlawed those!" said the governor.

"Yeah, you did, but I bought it a long time ago," replied the man. "By the way, Governor, the AR stands for ArmaLite Rifle, not an assault rifle. It's also not a fully automatic rifle. ArmaLite's the manufacturer's name. Not that it'll make any difference to you, but an automatic weapon keeps firing with one pull on the trigger until you take your finger off or run out of bullets. With this gun, you have to pull the trigger each time you want to shoot a single bullet." Shaking his head, the man said, "Sooo, you gave speeches and passed another law on something, and you don't even know what you were talking about."

"How many bullets can it shoot from that magazine?" asked the governor.

"This clip holds twenty. Yeah, I know you outlawed those too. Again, I bought this before stupidity took over," the man answered, his own irritation showing. "You know what, Governor, for a minute there, I had the foolish thought of putting you in the back room and telling you to run if any shooting started. I was going to try and defend myself and you if your kidnapping friends come looking for you. I don't think I'm going to do that."

"Just call the police!" demanded the governor.

"All right," the man said. "That's exactly what I'll do."

The worker punched in the numbers on his phone and told the dispatcher that he had a man in his store claiming to be the governor who said he had been kidnapped. The excitement on the other end of the line told the worker that his new visitor might be legitimate. The worker gave them all the information they asked for and then clicked the phone off. "They're sending help for you," the man said as he walked slowly toward the front door of the store with his rifle in hand. He carefully looked out of the windows and then approached the door, locked it, and shut off the open sign.

"What are you doing?" the governor asked.

Looking back at him for just a moment, the man said, "I don't want anyone coming in here! We won't know if they're good people or bad people until it's too late. At least if they break in with the door locked, we'll know immediately that they're not friendlies. If that happens, good luck to you."

"What do you mean by that?" asked the governor.

"Your troops are on the way," said the worker. "This is my store, and you can stay here if you want to wait on them."

"Wait, what are you going to do?" asked the governor in panic.

"I'm leaving," said the man.

"YOU'RE WHAT?" yelled the governor.

"You heard me. I'm leaving. I'll be somewhere nearby. I decided I'm not putting my life on the line for you. You've shown me you don't care about the rest of us regular folks. You know, those who don't have your security detail. You know, your security people, the ones who are all armed, by the way! So, why should I risk my life for yours? You don't think I should be able to defend myself, my family, or my business. I'm sure as hell not going to risk my life to save yours. Besides, if things do turn to shit, I might even have to defend myself in court for trying to do the right thing—for YOU! Hell, I could even get shot by your troops when they show up. They seem trigger-happy nowadays, you know?

"Nope," the man continued, "you're not worth it. Do you realize, Governor, you didn't even ask me my name? You just started ordering me around." With that, the man turned and walked toward the back of the store.

"Wait," said the governor. "Have you heard anything about my kids?"

"Why would I hear anything about your kids? I wouldn't know your kids if they walked in that door and called you Dad."

"Surely, there must have been something on the news about them? I need to know how they are!"

"Governor, I don't know anything about your kids."

"Are you saying there hasn't been anything on the news about them?"

"Not that I've seen. Why? Did they do something you think should have made the news?" With that, the man turned toward the back room.

"Wait; you can't leave. I'm the governor; you need to stay here. You'll be a hero," the governor said.

"To who?" asked the man. "Besides, that wouldn't mean much if I were dead, now, would it? I'll be close by in case someone shows up who's not the police. At least I can be a good witness. Isn't that what you want us private citizens to do? Don't intervene or defend ourselves. Just be a good witness to whatever horrible shit happens to some law-abiding citizen. This is what you wanted. You're getting what you wanted, Governor. Good luck!"

"Can you at least leave me your phone," the governor yelled at him.

The worker hesitated, then replied, as he walked away from him, "NO, I may need it to take a video of what happens to you so that your police can have something to go on for their investigation. Besides, your guys would probably take it away from me. I'd never get it back! I can't afford another one." Walking briskly, the man went through the door to the back room.

The governor heard a door open and close. The governor rushed back, found the door, closed it, and locked it. He returned to the front of the store and crouched down behind the counter. Off to his left, he saw several shelves of snacks, the sight of which reminded him how hungry he was. He crawled over and pulled several items from the shelf and then saw a tall cooler with some sodas in it. He grabbed a bottle and started back toward his hiding place when he heard a truck pull up in front. He scrambled back behind the counter and slowly peeked up over it. A man in a big heavy coat walked toward the door and tried to open it. When it didn't open, he leaned forward and looked into the store; he tried the door again, stepped back, and looked side to side. Then he looked again at the unlit "OPEN" sign hanging darkly in the window and again tried the door. When the door didn't budge, he shrugged, walked back to his truck, and drove off.

Weak with relief, the governor opened the snacks and started devouring them. It had been a long time since the worker had called the police, and he was getting scared. If someone was looking for him, he would not be hard to find. From what he had seen, this was about the only place that was out here. The dead car would be a giveaway, too. He didn't have much choice about staying in the store or leaving. He felt the store was an island of safety, and this was where the police would be looking for him.

After several more minutes, he could hear the sirens off in the distance. His breath left him in relief. He was going to be ok now. The sirens grew louder. Then he could hear cars fast approaching and cornering into the parking area out front. He slowly looked up and saw two uniformed figures with guns drawn exit their cars and settle down behind them, putting protection between themselves and whatever was inside the store.

The governor stood and waved his arms and started to move toward the front of the store. "STOP RIGHT THERE!" one of the uniforms commanded.

The governor kept moving and yelled, "IT'S ME! I'M THE GOVERNOR!"

"DON'T TAKE ANOTHER STEP," was the next command.

He stopped moving.

"Are you alone?" the officer yelled.

"YES!" replied the governor.

With guns still aimed at the governor, the officer commanded him to walk slowly toward the door and keep his hands up. He walked toward the door and stopped as he reached it. The officer commanded him to come outside.

"I have to put my hands down to unlock the door," the governor yelled back.

"Ok, do it slowly, one hand only!"

As he reached down to unlock the door, another police car screeched to a stop out front, followed by another. He stopped after unlocking the door. He put his hands back up and stood there. He could see the officers were communicating about what to do next.

"Step outside slowly and approach the car on your far right. Keep your hands up," came the command.

As he took small steps, following the orders, another car pulled up. Officers were putting on protective equipment and were now armed with rifles. An officer behind the far-right car motioned for him to move toward him as another officer came up next to the one giving the orders. "Turn around now and walk backward toward us."

He did as he was told, and then he felt hands upon him, searching him. When they were done, they told him to get down beside them behind the car. "Is there anyone else in there?" they asked.

"No, someone who worked there was there, but he left. He's somewhere out there," he said, pointing to the woods in the distance. "He said he'd be watching from where it was safe."

One of the officers spoke into the radio mic connected to their shirt, and another team of officers with rifles leveled toward the building approached the front door while two others went around back. On a command, they entered the building. After several minutes, they all came back toward their cars, lowering their weapons and letting the adrenaline dissipate from their bodies.

Another siren came screaming down the road, and an ambulance appeared in the parking lot, followed by a news van. The officers motioned to the paramedics to follow them as they guided the governor back inside the store and away from the news people. As the paramedics examined the governor, a ranking officer arrived and took charge of the unfolding situation. She introduced herself to the governor and told him she was the OSC, the on-scene commander. After asking the governor how he was doing and dealing with some preliminaries, she began asking the governor questions: "Do you know who did this?"

Without answering, the governor interrupted the officer, "How are my kids?"

"Your kids are fine," said the OSC. "We've had them and your wife secured and well-guarded since you disappeared."

"But what about the attack on my daughter?"

"Governor, there's been no attack on your daughter!"

"What, how can that be? Are you sure? What about my son? Do you know what happened to him?"

The officer, starting to get worried that something may have happened that she didn't know about, said, "Governor, as far as I know, your wife and both of your kids are safe. They're worried about you, but they're ok."

"Can you check on them? Please! I just need to know they're all right."

Nodding yes, the officer spoke into her radio and asked the person on the other end to do a check with the unit protecting the governor's family to make sure nothing had happened that she was not aware of. "Governor, our folks will get back to us in a few moments. Just take it easy. We'll make sure they're safe.

"Let's get back to you for now," the OSC said and began a line of questions. "Do you know who did this to you?" "Do you know why they did this?" "Can you tell us where you were?" "How many people were there?" "Were you harmed?" "Did they make any demands?" "Did you recognize anything that could help us find them?" "How did you wind up here?" He gave her as much information as he could as quickly as he could, but that last question struck him as maybe the most helpful. "I woke up in a car. I think it's maybe a few miles down that small road from here. I walked from it to here. Maybe that can help."

The OSC told one of the other officers to go check the car and see what they could find. "Treat the car and the surrounding area as a crime scene. Get forensics here to go over it, too. Then, get it towed in and checked over again for any evidence."

The governor told them, "It's electric, and it's dead."

As the other officer was starting to walk away to do what he was told, the OSC called after him, "When you're ready, call for a tow truck and have it hauled in. Tell the tow people that it's electric; those electric vehicles require a special tow vehicle."

The OSC's radio came to life, reporting that the governor's family was safe and secure. Nothing had happened. There were no attacks on either child. "Your family's all doing fine and greatly relieved at the news of your escape," she told the governor. Leaning in closer for some bit of privacy amid the surrounding chaos, she added, "They send their love and say they cannot wait to see you."

As the OSC attempted to continue her questioning of the governor, an officer approached the OSC to tell her a helicopter was on its way to pick up the governor. Shortly after, another officer interrupted the questioning and told the OSC, "There's a guy outside who says he owns this place and wants to come in and see if there's any damage to his store. He also wants to see how the governor's doing. I've verified he's the owner. He says his name's Sam."

The governor looked outside and said, "Yeah, that's the guy who was here."

The OSC told the officer to search him. "Make sure he's not carrying a weapon before he comes in."

"We already did. He's clean," said the officer.

Sam came in and started to look around. He saw the governor. "I guess it worked out for you, didn't it?" Sam said. Looking at the empty wrappers and soda bottle, he continued, "I see you helped yourself to some of my products."

The governor started to say something, but the OSC interrupted, "We're going to close your place down while we conduct our investigation. We're going to have to ask you some questions."

"Why do you need to shut me down?" asked Sam.

"For now, I'm looking at this as a potential crime scene," said the OSC. "Go with this officer, and they'll get started with your interview." As Sam walked away with the officer, the OSC told the governor, "We'll have to look deep into him."

"Why?" the governor asked. "He didn't do anything that I know of."

"You never know; he might be part of this," the OSC replied.

The noise of the helicopter's arrival interrupted all discussions. As it touched down, the OSC escorted the governor to it and helped him aboard. "Go on back, get some food and rest. Take care of yourself for a few days before you get back to work. My boss will be waiting for you to take your statements and get the investigation going. We'll let him know what we find out here." With that, the OSC and the governor nodded at each other. The governor was situated aboard the helicopter by the crew. The OSC moved to a safe distance and watched the helicopter lift from the parking lot and disappear over the trees.

# PART III

A few days later, the commander of the state police was in the governor's office, briefing the governor on the status of the investigation. "I am sorry to say, Governor, but we're hitting dead ends on just about every aspect of what happened.

"As you are aware, we believe the scenarios involving your daughter and son were either actors paid to play those roles or AI-generated productions. Our guess at this time is that they were AI-generated. The backgrounds would be easy to copy from just about anywhere. We have a team of specialists using sophisticated software searching the internet to identify that locker room. The town scene could have come from any number of sources and then regenerated with those people in the scene. Facial recognition searches haven't generated much, either. Especially because they used your kids' own faces. Those were probably lifted off social media and then artificially manipulated for their intended purpose. We've not come up with anything on the other two people in the two scenes. Our experts believe they were AI-generated as well. They also said that according to your description of the poor quality of the screen you were viewing them on, whoever made them was counting on the images to be close enough to reality for you to believe what you were seeing. They didn't have to be perfect."

"Maybe not," said the governor, "but they were good enough. I believed it. I don't ever want to see something like that again. I still see those images and probably will for the rest of my life."

"Let's be thankful that what you saw didn't really happen to them. There are parents out there who could only wish what happened to their kids wasn't real," said the commander.

"If it's ok, I'll go on with the next part," said the commander. "It's obvious you were drugged somehow, both right before you were taken and again before you were put in the car you woke up in. Toxicology is still working on it. They used some kind of unique drug on you during the initial capture. It had to be something fast-acting but one that would also keep you knocked out until they got you to wherever they kept you. Same thing on the other end, at the end of your captivity. Whoever did it knew what they were doing. It required some chemical or medical knowledge to pick the right drug to do what it did and make the timing work for them. Whoever did all this was very sophisticated and knew how to cover their tracks."

"The guy at the store seems to be clean; in fact, he's a retired police officer," continued the commander. "He has no priors and, as far as we can tell, doesn't have any affiliations with any groups we'd normally suspect in a situation like this. So far, the only thing he's guilty of is not being a fan of yours. But we're still digging. He's probably regretting not helping you more when he had the chance. His life would be a lot easier and less complicated now."

"What about the car, any clues there?" asked the governor.

"Nope, the car itself was stolen. That situation gets a little compli-cated," the commander said.

"What do you mean?" the governor asked.

"The car belonged to a married guy with a couple of kids. He said he was coming out of a supermarket, and as he started to get in his car, another car pulled up behind him, and two guys got out, one with a gun, and demanded his keys. He says he was so scared he dropped his groceries. He got his keys out and gave them over. They pushed him down, kicked him, and told him to stay down till they were gone, or they'd shoot him. The surveillance cameras at the store support his version of his story."

"Then what's complicated about it?" asked the governor.

"Well," said the commander, "this is where it gets interesting. We have surveillance video on this, too. A short time later, after stealing the car from the guy shopping, these same two guys in the stolen car pull up in front of a convenience store. Suspect #1 stays in the car, and the passenger, suspect #2, goes into the store, empties the cash register, and starts grabbing baskets full of stuff. While he's in the store, robbing it, two guys walk up to the driver's side of the stolen car parked out front of the store. I'll call these two people suspects #3 and #4. Suspect #3 opens the driver's side door of the stolen car, unsnaps the seat belt, and pulls the driver out. As he does so, he grabs the top of suspect #1's hoodie and pulls it down off his shoulder to about his elbows so the guy can't move. As a side note, Governor, maybe one of the things you should add to your list of things to ban is hoodies. They're used in almost every street crime committed.

"Anyway," the commander continued, "Suspect #3 kicks suspect #1's legs out from under him and puts him face down on the asphalt. In the meantime, suspect #4 slides into the driver's seat of the stolen car and backs the car up. He maneuvers it so the passenger side door is angled near his partner."

The governor interrupted, "What do you make of these second two people, suspects 3 & 4?"

"Well, again, it's interesting," said the commander. "They're stealing a stolen car from people who stole it in the first place. So, yes, they're bad guys, too, but what the hell are they doing stealing a car from other bad guys? We don't know! There are a few possibilities. One, they were either in on what happened to you; two, they didn't know they were stealing a stolen car; or 3, maybe they're from a rival gang or group. We just don't know yet. We're operating on the theory that the second two guys were in on what happened to you because the car didn't show up again until you woke up in it."

"So, anyway, suspect # 3 pulls suspect #1 off the asphalt, says something to him, and kicks him in the ass. Suspect #1 takes off running and goes around behind the store. Suspect #4, who's now behind the wheel of a stolen car, pulls up beside his partner, and the partner, suspect #3, slides into the passenger seat. These second two people, #3 and #4, drive off in the now re-stolen car.

"Right after that," said the commander, "suspect #2 comes out of the store with his baskets full of freshly stolen stuff, but there's no car, and his partner, who he arrived with, is gone. He just takes off running down the street with his stolen goods. Him, we got. He has a long record, multiple arrests, and three prior felony convictions: armed robbery, illegal possession of a firearm, and felony assault. He shouldn't even be out on the street. The prosecutors and the judges just keep turning him loose.

"Again," said the commander, "there's no connecting him with anything else we're looking into regarding your situation. We're still looking for suspect #1, but we'll find him because of his connection to his partner in crime. We can't find anything on suspects #3 and #4. They were fully covered by their clothes and gloves. They didn't have anything visible or distinguishing to help identify them. I'd guess, though, that those second two guys had some specialized training in taking people down and restraining them. I'd say they were, at some point, either law enforcement, military, or both. They were quick and decisive. They knew exactly what they were doing and how to do it. They worked as a very effective team. We're checking to see if there have been any other incidents using similar tactics."

The commander continued, "The owner of the car is being investigated as well. So far, same thing, no connection to any groups that we're aware of, but we'll keep digging into them."

"Them?" asked the governor. "Is it a family car?"

"Yes," said the commander, "a traditional mom, dad, two teenagers. He's a first-level manager at a factory, and she's a teacher. We pretty much took the car apart but didn't find anything there either."

The governor sat quietly for a minute and then asked the commander, "Have they got their car back yet?"

"No, we impounded it until we're ready to release it," the commander said.

"What are they doing for a car in the meantime?" asked the governor.

"That's not our problem, Governor. Maybe they got a rental."

"Who pays for that?" asked the governor.

The commander looked inquisitively at the governor, "Well, if they have insurance, their insurance may cover it, at least for a while, and then it will be on the owners to pay it. Again, not our problem."

"When will the car be released?" asked the governor.

"I haven't decided yet. Maybe when we're done investigating them, in the unlikely event that we do turn up something," the commander replied.

"So, let me get this straight," the governor said, leaning forward in his chair. "A family has their car stolen. It was used in a crime, but a crime they have no known connection to. We've checked the car, and nothing of value to the investigation was found. Is that correct?" He looked at the commander.

The commander nodded in agreement.

"How much is the impound cost?" the governor asked.

"It could be several hundred dollars," said the commander. "Their insurance will probably pay it, but, again, that's not our problem."

"But it's a problem for them. I'd guess a big problem," said the governor. "What happens to the car if they can't pay to get it out of the compound?"

The commander responded, "Well, after fifteen days, the car basically belongs to the impound company, and they can sell it or auction the car off. Why are you worried about this, Governor?"

"Let me ask you a question, Commander. Who represents the family in this situation?" the governor asked.

The commander shrugged, "I guess they can hire a lawyer."

The governor was astonished. "At more expense to them?"

"Well, yes, that's the way it works. And remember, Governor, we're still investigating them. That's the way the laws on these things work, Governor; I thought you were familiar with the process," the commander stated.

"Yeah, I should be," said the governor. "I just haven't had much personal experience with things like this until recently." He looked at the commander. "Can you release the car from impound and just call the family to come and get it?"

"No, I can't," said the commander. "That's not the way the law works. The state, and most cities, have contracts with the towing and impound companies that are legally binding."

The governor said, "All of it to the benefit of the state, cities, and most of all to the towing and impound companies, right?"

"Yes, pretty much," said the commander, "but there are laws and regulations. Respectfully, sir, that IS MY job, to enforce the laws. If YOU want things to be different, Governor, then it's your job to fix them. The folks in law enforcement see these things every day. The people that get involved with our courts and criminal justice system for crimes they did or did not do are usually punished further by our own systems."

"What do you mean the people who get involved in our courts and criminal system get punished by our systems?" asked the governor.

The commander shifted in his chair, looked directly at the governor, and said, "We've basically legitimized punishing people because they're poor or just regular middle-class people who had some misfortune that put them in our legal system. Your office, the legislature, and the courts have made those actions we take against them legal as part of the system. I know they're not technically crimes in the general sense; they're more like crimes against humanity, at least the poor segments of humanity. In fact, once something happens to poor people, and they get caught up in this system of ours, they're trapped, and it's expensive. In this case, the family the car was stolen from is going to pay a lot of money just because they were the victims of a crime.

"In other cases where someone's been charged with a crime, not found guilty yet, just charged, they pay too, only for different reasons and in different ways. But, respectfully, Governor, you should probably ask one of your prosecutors, your attorney general, or one of your legal experts who you trust these questions instead of me. However, I'll just say that if someone violates a law or is suspected of violating a law, unless it's murder, there really is no investigation. Law enforcement takes statements and files a report, but there's no thorough investigation. Law enforcement arrests them, and we're pretty much done with it. Of course, our officers appear in court and testify when required, but unless it's a major crime or a crime that happens to someone with a high profile, like yourself, we're out of it.

"Then," continued the commander, "depending on what they've done, the prosecutor will charge them with everything they can and then add more charges on top of those charges. They do that so that the charged person will have to plead guilty at some point to something. They must either take a plea deal or risk going in front of a jury that assumes they're guilty in the first place, or they wouldn't be in court. Even if a person is put on trial and charged with the more serious crime the prosecutor put on them, if the prosecutor sees the jury isn't buying their version of the case at the more serious level, the prosecutor can drop the charges down to a lesser one that they think has a greater chance of delivering a guilty verdict. The prosecutor does not have to stick with the original charge; it can be changed at any time during the trial. If your objective is a guilty verdict, that's a great system. If your objective is justice, that seems a little less than fair to the accused, don't you think? Once the accused agrees to a plea deal, that plea goes into the 'win' column for the prosecution and the public, and all is right with the world. Another bad person has been punished, RIGHT?!

"Just to put a finer point on it, Governor, until they plea, the process at this stage is just a verbal contest between two lawyers in a room with a judge who usually agrees with the prosecutor. If the accused can't afford a non-public defender—and I mean, who can? —they get an overworked public defender who, with the best of intentions, with a large caseload, and to the best of their ability, will spend about ten minutes with them out in the hall on the day of their hearing before they go into court. On top of that, there is a shortage of public defenders. The accused may have to wait days or weeks to be assigned a public defender. The whole system is set up as a production system, not a justice system. The prosecutors' rule without restraint!

"I apologize, Governor, for being so verbal, but this is important. The old rule of innocent until proven guilty has been long dead, except for a small portion of the population. If you're accused, you're guilty. The defendants in the criminal courts must prove they are innocent. Again, who has the money to do that? Poor and middle-class people cannot afford expert or technical witnesses or pay the additional hourly cost of good and thorough representation. No, the small folks that I see caught up in the grinding wheels of our system are screwed."

"If it's so bad, why do you do the job you're doing?" asked the governor.

"When I started, it wasn't like it is now," replied the commander. "It's become this way over the last several years. When I started, we were allowed to use judgment in an arrest for nonviolent crimes. We often were able to work things out between folks having a problem. I think because we did a pretty good job of that, we didn't have the backlog in the court system the way you do now. We also have a lot more laws now and a lot more rules that say we must make an arrest. We didn't have to deal with the level of disrespect for the rule of law and lack of basic civility that prevails today. I'm not on the street anymore like I was. I don't see it firsthand as much, but my officers do. The system takes a personal toll on everyone touched by it. Law enforcement gets criticized from all angles. Citizens don't respect us, the courts use us for their purposes, and the media and the organized groups trying to break down the structures of our society use everything they can against us. I know we, as law enforcement, make mistakes now and then, but overall, we do a damn good job. I didn't think about it until you just asked me that question about why I'm still doing the job, but sitting here, I realized I see a lot of bad people, people who deserve the fullest application of our rules and processes. I get a tremendous amount of personal satisfaction when that happens. But I also see the others, the ones I've been talking about; there's no one speaking for them. They have no voice. Even though it may be strange coming from someone like me, I hope I have enough credibility with you, from my experience, from the performance of my job on a daily basis, that you can trust what I'm telling you and that you take my words seriously."

"I find some of what you're telling me hard to believe, Commander," said the governor. "For years, the people made it very clear that they wanted criminals punished. I know you know, Commander, that's how the 'Three Strikes and You're Out' laws came into being. In the last few years, you also know we've worked hard to reform police processes to reduce the disparate treatment inherent in our system to correct these injustices. Are you telling me they're not working?"

The commander said, "I know some people like to call the changes made to the system 'reforms,' but there's been no 'reform.' No detailed look at the criminal justice system and how it works. Not in a way that would allow people who aren't familiar with the system to see what really happens daily. The way 'reform' works now is that some vocal people or groups of people make charges against the system. They and their advocates cherry-pick statistics and antidotes. Then, the people who understand the system the least, the legislature, make changes to appease the vocal ones. That's not reform; it's giving a pass to destructive criminal behavior in the name of social justice. I can testify that there are a lot of bad people out there, and, ironically, the same system that punishes everyday working people releases habitual repeat offenders, even those who have committed the most serious crimes, back onto the street to go do the same things over, and over, again. We just arrest them again. Then they're back out. All through the same system. That's not a justice system."

"What do you mean when you say the system punishes people unnecessarily?" asked the governor. "I don't see how that's happening!"

"Well, again, I recommend you talk to your attorney general, but it seems to me that for a good portion of the court caseload, someone just made a mistake. There are so many laws now that it's very easy to commit a 'crime.' They're locked up or put on an ankle bracelet restricted to their homes, if they have a home, before their case goes to trial. Cases are continued repeatedly. The accused and all involved often show up, and if the accused is fortunate enough to have a job, they miss work to show up at the courthouse to find out their day in court's been delayed, often multiple times. In addition to missing work, they may have paid for parking and if they do have a private attorney, they more than likely pay the attorney for the hours of their time for showing up. There is no such thing as a speedy trial. After a while, they may even enter a plea just to get it over with. I wonder if you know that, across this country, there are a tremendous number of suicides in jails by people waiting to have their cases resolved. They're killing themselves and haven't even been found guilty of a crime. For those waiting for their case to be resolved outside of jail, some are allowed to work, and others are not. Then, the system finds them guilty, applies fines, and charges court costs for what they did or because they had to plead to something they did not do. Many of these folks are just working people, often the working poor, who made a mistake. When they can't pay the fines, the courts add interest and more fines on top of it. Then maybe their driver's license gets suspended because they didn't pay some fine or other court-imposed costs. Then they can't go to work. They can't put food on the table or pay their bills, their credit's trashed, and then we punish them some more. If they plead guilty to a charge or go before a jury and are found guilty, they are going to have a hard time finding another job. How do they provide food and shelter for themselves or their family? We put them in a no-win situation. We pile punishments onto the poor in ways that lead to desperation and possibly more crime and more cost to society. It's a shame. There must be a better way."

The governor stood up to signal the meeting was over. "Thank you for sharing the update and your reality with me," said the governor. "I think there's a lot of work that needs to be done to rebalance this state for not just some of the people but all of them."

"I agree," said the commander.

As the commander got up to leave, he told the governor he would keep him updated on the investigation as it progressed. He started toward the office door, turned to the governor, and said, "I know there are certainly a lot of things for you to think about in your job, but I encourage you to put some effort into this one. Civil society is falling apart. It's not going to be easy, Governor; some REAL leadership is going to be needed. It's not like you're an emperor or something like that, ruling by divine right. You're going to get a lot of resistance from a lot of people who've made a career out of advocacy for special interest groups. You'll also get pushback from the people who control those systems and from those people who don't know how the systems work because they've never had any experience with them. How about being the advocate for all the state's citizens? You could make a very big difference and possibly prevent a lot worse things that are coming. A new plan would be welcomed by ALL of us."

The commander turned and walked out of the office door. "Wait a minute," said the governor. "Why did you say that about me not being an emperor? Where did that come from?"

The commander hesitated and replied, "You told us during the investigation that the voice said that's what some people call you. You said you were very clear to him that you didn't think of yourself that way, that you were a leader. We just hope you're up to the challenge." He nodded to the governor and walked away.

The governor stood staring at the empty doorway where the commander had just stood, his final comments playing on his mind. Trying to come to grips with the unsettling feelings moving through him. He sat back down at his desk, asking himself: what did he really mean by that statement? Did the commander see him the same way as the voice saw him?

Pushing his discomfort from the discussion with the commander, especially his last comments, to the back of his mind, the governor leaned back in his chair and reflected on all that he had been through in the last few weeks. He picked up a piece of paper and wrote "ISSUES" across the top. He started making a list on the empty page. When he was done, he folded the piece of paper and put it in his suit coat pocket. Throughout the day and evening, he pulled the paper out to modify it, drawing a line through some things, adding others, and clarifying other points. By the time he was done, he had filled three more pages with notes.

The next morning, he handed his chief of staff two pieces of paper during their meeting. The first one had the words: "TAXES, FEES, FINES, & PENALTIES" across the top of the page. Written beneath the title were two columns. The first column was labeled; "CATEGORY." The second asked the question, "WHERE DOES THE MONEY GO?" The first column of the paper was populated with a list of fifteen taxes, fines, fees, and other penalties that the governor had listed. The second was blank.

Across the top of the second piece of paper was the title: "LAWS AND REGULATIONS CHALLENGED DURING THE LAST EIGHT YEARS."

The governor said, "I need your help. I want to understand a couple of issues thoroughly, and I need help to do that. I want a complete list of all the taxes, fees, fines, and penalties that are placed upon the citizens of this state. I think I'm familiar with most of the taxes affecting income, but maybe I don't know as much as I think I do. So, I want a complete list of everything that we tax related to income, investments, inheritance, transfers of money of any kind between people or businesses, and anything and everything related. I also want to know which state fund each category of those moneys goes into.

"I also want an exhaustive list of those things that you see meeting those criteria of fees, fines, and penalties. Some items like court costs, court fines, and fees can be put under the heading of courts. Construction, building, code enforcement, and that kind of thing can be grouped under their own category.

"I know this one will sound like small stuff, but I want to know all the costs associated with having a person's car towed and impounded. How does law enforcement get involved in the towing and impounding of vehicles? How much are impounding fees? What are the laws and rules regarding that whole process? I think this one may be indicative of how a part of our system works and its impact on the poor and others. Do you understand what I'm asking for?"

The chief of staff sat looking at the two sheets of paper, then said, "What's going on, Governor?"

"I'm not sure even we know what's going on!" said the governor. "That's the point. I don't believe we've ever stood back and looked at what we're doing and how much it's costing our citizens. I do know that we always need money to fund our agencies, the courts, and the solutions to the problems we see, but how are we doing it? Where does the money reside in the budget? Where does the money actually go? I just want to understand it.

"That next page, the one about laws and regulations challenged in the last eight years, I want to understand what our most controversial laws and regulations were. I think anything with a legal challenge would fit that criterion. Anything that the press, the business community, or any other organization took exception to would also meet that criterion. I'm looking for patterns. What was the pressing need that made it necessary? In effect, why did we pass or enact it? Who did it help? Who did it harm? Who was behind the law or regulations? By that, I mean organizations, companies, or lobbyists. Or us? Who? Most importantly, I want to know: can we prove that it solved the problem it was intended to?"

"Governor," said his chief, "this is going to be a tremendous amount of work."

"I know, but I want it done. I have a suggestion. I'm looking at this as a research project. Instead of hiring lawyers, consultants, or interns, which will cost us money, how about canvasing the cabinet, and seeing if they have some people in our departments with the skills needed who could be loaned to you to form a team for the duration of this project? Also, I want you to ask the colleges if they have a cross-section of business, political science, organization studies, STEM majors, or other disciplines that you can think of who they would recommend for this project. It would be a good experience for them. If they agree, tell them I want them to pay for the student's time out of the college's budget. After all, they are state-funded schools with large endowments. We shouldn't have to pay them twice. You can also check with private colleges to see if they want to participate. One more thing: whoever is nominated, I want them screened and approved by your office first. I want a cross-section of every category of person, especially diverse political and societal opinions. Once you have screened them and selected the groups, I want to talk to them as a group before they get the final go-ahead.

"I also want you and your staff to think of what is causing my administration, our processes, and systems to be a thorn in the people's side. These are things that you all hear the most complaints about. Focus on the lower-earning people and middle class of ALL colors and ethnicities. DO NOT focus on just one group. Not just minorities, not just ethnicities. I want you to think about the general population, from the unemployed up to the middle class. I want to see a list of everything that doesn't make sense to those people, from environmental regulations, law enforcement, laws, and court processes. Don't look at it through our eyes; I want you to look at these things through their eyes, the ones that are being affected the most. I want to know the things that hurt them financially or have a disproportionate impact on the middle to lower rungs of our economy and population. I want it by the strata groups that I mentioned. Do you understand what I'm asking for?"

The chief of staff said, "I'm not sure I do, Governor. Everything we do or have put in place has been for a reason. We are serving our constituencies."

The governor said, "I'm sure we think so. If your group cannot find anything that should be on that list, then perhaps we may be part of the problem. If that's the case, I want you to go create a process to find a cross-section of people who were, or that you think might be, impacted by the things I've listed and see what they think or want to put on that list. I don't want it by party affiliations, either. I want a true cross-section of the population. If you cannot do that, find a non-partisan consulting outfit with a good impartial reputation and have them look at it. Either way, I want some answers."

The chief nodded in the affirmative.

The governor continued, "I also want a meeting with our environmental and energy-related committee chairs and our environmental and energy agency leadership. After we hold that meeting and learn what we learn, I'll want a separate meeting with the heads of the financial management committee. I have some questions for them also," said the governor.

"What kind of questions?" asked the chief of staff.

"From the environmental people, I want to understand the measurable differences we've made in our own environmental numbers over the last twenty years. How has our work impacted the numbers on a state and on a global scale? What is the actual impact of what we've been doing? From the financial people, I want to know at what cost to our population, financially, and to their way of life?"

"Help me understand, Governor," interjected the chief of staff. "On this one, what do you want to know?"

The governor said, "I'm sure, or at least I hope, that your investigation will find we've made great strides in water quality and improvement in localized air quality for our own state. I want to see graph lines from when we started taking environmental issues seriously until now. How are we doing? On another chart, I want to see projected lines that show how what we're doing now will impact those numbers in the future, both for our state and for the planet as a whole. I want to see projected costs overlaid with that information. Are we just a tail, wagging a dog, and punishing our own people while others are feeling empowered to continue to pollute as we force sacrifices on our own people for no perceptible difference other than it makes us feel better about ourselves? Don't get me wrong, I don't want to stop making improvements to either the local or the global environments when it's justified, and I believe it can be. I want to make sure we're making the difference we think we're making. We cannot clean up the world single-handedly on the backs of our state's citizens. If our efforts boil down to that, I want a different plan. Maybe, just maybe, there are other avenues that should be looked at that could make a bigger difference."

"Governor," the chief of staff cautioned, "the people doing this work and formulating these plans already believe they are making a difference. They believe the plans and programs they have, and are, putting in place are necessary to the future of the state and the planet, or they wouldn't be doing them."

"I understand that they believe that," said the governor. "I want to make sure we really have a plan that will hold up to the reality of what we say we're doing. If that turns out to be the case, maybe we have not been doing a very good job of educating and bringing the public along with us. Regardless, we still need to know what can we pay for without bankrupting our population and the state? It will be great if our people can answer those questions to my satisfaction. But it's going to be on you and me to make sure our environmental and financial staff know they're going to put that data and that plan in front of me, and eventually both houses of the legislative and joint committees, on a regular basis to see how we're doing against their plans and their cost estimates. I want the information released as public information.

"Those making the plans and managing them will be accountable for the integrity of their data and the results," stated the governor. "Also, while you're at it, I want to talk to somebody about how we go about truly understanding what's happening in our court system."

"What are you looking for on that item?" asked the chief of staff.

"I know I don't want to see the same reports about disparate treatment of races. We know that data. I want to see the data cut by economic level for one thing. I've heard about a study that was conducted several years ago that showed that there is a difference in outcomes of interaction with the courts in criminal cases depending upon the accused's financial situation.

"But, Governor, we know that the data shows disparate treatment and impacts by race; that issue's not going to go away."

"Look, I've given this a lot of thought," said the governor. "I'm not trying to downplay or say that the issue of racial discrimination is not a problem. It is. I want that issue addressed. We need an improved system for everyone. Some people like to say that our country is supposed to have the best system in the world. That may or may not be true. My opinion is that our system is not good enough. It is not worthy of what, and who, we as a nation aspire to be. One thing I've realized is that we have several different levels of criminal justice and legal systems at work in this state and country. We all have been solely focused on addressing just one of them."

"Can you help me understand that, Governor?"

"Absolutely, there is a lot of information that people of color get treated poorly in our legal system. That is one group. But poor people regardless of race, sex, gender, and ethnicity, can also become victims of the system. That is another group. They just don't get the attention, nor do they have multiple advocacy groups raising the issues on their behalf. I believe that all those groups get treated differently by our court systems compared with those who can afford necessary legal representation. Another group is people who can afford representation. Even though it may be financially painful to the people in that group they can at least try to defend themselves, but at what costs? Then, there is even another group on a whole different level: the wealthy, elites, the famous, and the politically connected, who get treated in a totally different and preferential way to the other groups. They can pay for the best lawyers and experts available.

"Some people argue that you only get 'justice' if you can afford to pay for it. We've not been listening to the ones who cannot afford it. Who speaks for them? Most of the people in this country cannot afford the same level of justice and representation that the rich and powerful can. We used to call ourselves a nation of laws, and I guess that is still true. But I understand a lot better now why some call what we have an 'injustice' system. How can it be called a justice system when the accused's financial ability to defend themselves is the determining factor of the treatment or 'justice' they receive? How do we fix that?

"Then on the flip side," continued the governor. "There's all this crime going on that's destroying our communities and businesses. People aren't safe in their own homes, walking in their own neighborhoods, or going into their towns. Why are these violent criminals being arrested and released? I know some think this is ok now, but it's not! It's seriously eroded people's confidence in the government and the institutions they used to respect that helped keep them safe. In fact, many clearly see that the government is creating these problems and allowing them to proliferate. How is that justice? Why is this happening? What do we do about it? These are the things I want to know.

"I want to know how it all works. I want to start another research project into these issues. I want someone as impartial as you can find to lead it. Someone I can talk to who will understand what I want done. Someone who will get it done! Tell them they will make many powerful enemies, but we'll give them our support! By the time you find me someone, I'll have figured out exactly what I want to know and what I'm looking for. Got it?"

"Yes, sir, got it!" said the chief. "But I think you're going to run into some major internal political issues with this one, Governor."

"In what way?" asked the governor.

"As you know, Governor, the operation of the courts falls under the chief justice of the state supreme court, and then there's the court administrator who reports to the chief justice. Her office of state court administration is responsible for the operation of the court system."

"Yeah, I know," said the governor. "You and I will work those boundary lines. We can tell them we're looking into some issues and will share the information with them and involve them in the project design and our findings."

"We also have multiple justice-related legislative committees," said the chief, "that are going to feel their toes are being stepped on."

"Yeah, ok, I understand; you're right. I should meet with those committee chairs and the court administrator and involve them in what I see needs to be taken a good hard look at. I still want someone to head this as a project, and I want someone reporting directly to me," said the governor.

"Governor, it's the job of the court administrator to be the liaison between your office, the chief justice, and the legislature. If not handled well, it will be a problem for you. Your project could get sabotaged before it gets started."

"Good point," said the governor. "How about we leave the committee chairs out of it for now? Set up a meeting among you, the court administrator, and me, and let's discuss this issue. However, just to be clear, I want to present a proposal at that meeting that we proceed with the research project with the court administrator and a person reporting directly to me as co-chairs of the project."

"That might work, Governor. What do you think of having the lieutenant governor in the role of co-chair?"

The governor thought for a moment and said, "I know that should be the natural go-to role for this job, but I worry about the political optics. We're of the same party and have been aligned on almost everything we've done. I want this not to look like business as usual because it won't be. I want people to see that we're trying to get outside of our ideological boxes. Give it some thought and get back to me with a short list of names of the co-chairs, and then we can talk further. In the meantime, set up our meeting with the court administrator; let's see how that first step goes; will you please?"

"I will, but I must say, Governor, that with everything else you have going on, you're taking on a lot! Are you sure you're up for this ride? It will be a turbulent one?" said the chief.

The governor looked at him for a moment before he answered, "Yes! I am. If I'm going to hold this job and lead this state, I want to do the best job I can for all its people, me included."

"Yes, sir," said the chief as he nodded his head, rose from his chair, and began his exit from the office.

On their way out, the chief of staff passed the governor's office administrator on their way into his office. "Governor, your next appointment is here," said the administrator.

"Thank you, send them in. We have a lot of work to do," said the governor.

# EPILOGUE

S hortly after the governor's reappearance, the FBI entered the investigation, but not by invitation, as is normal in a kidnapping. There was a significant dispute among state law enforcement as to whether the FBI should be invited to investigate the case. The attorney general, who wanted to be the next governor of the state, adamantly wanted the FBI involved. She thought it would be a win for her if they were in or out.

The FBI's involvement would give her some added visibility with the press, connections with Washington DC, and credibility at the national level. Not that she would be lacking in visibility if it remained a state issue. She was, after all, the top law enforcement official in the state hierarchy. It would be her holding the press conferences and calling the shots. The downside would be if the perpetrators were not found. That would not look good for her political future. In that case, if the FBI were involved, the failure to find the perpetrators would fall upon the shoulders of the FBI, not hers.

State operational and investigative law enforcement were clear that they did not want or need the FBI's version of leadership. The FBI had not had a string of brilliant successes of late. It seemed that everything they touched turned into a scandal of ineptitude and politicization. State law enforcement argued that this was their governor, their state, and they wanted to own the investigation.

The FBI, because it was such a high-profile case, wanted it under their purview. The case had all the merits that the leaders in Washington were drooling over. Most importantly, a progressive governor had been kidnapped. They could not have wished for a better plum of a case to be dropped into their laps. They could bury the opposition for years to come with just the accusatory headlines alone, true or not, that they could generate based on this one case. A case of this type would give them justification to continue eroding the individual freedoms protected by the Constitution and the Bill of Rights. It would also pave the path to intrude more into every aspect of what, at one time, was the privacy of American citizens' lives.

In the end, it was, as usual, a political, not procedural, decision. The president, the attorney general of the US, the heads of Homeland Security, the FBI, and the CIA pressured the governor to include the FBI in the investigation.

The investigation used every method available to track people to find suspects. The National Security Agency combed through their numerous and massive data center warehouses containing data from every citizen of this country's phone and electronic messaging systems. The FBI and CIA worked with their partners at the large social media companies using algorithms to scour every post and message that had been exchanged from a year before the kidnapping until months after the reappearance of the governor. Whoever was involved in the taking of the governor was very much aware of the government's search capabilities. Whoever they were, they had avoided leaving an electronic trail for anyone to follow.

It was assumed that it must have been a very tight-knit, small group of people. They had maintained communication discipline. Nothing was leaked that could be provided to law enforcement in a way that would allow them to infiltrate the group. Nothing was found.

After all the publicity and fanfare over jurisdiction, the investigation quietly wound down. No evidence of significance could be found. Because of that fact alone, conspiracy theories started to appear. The most prominent posited that the federal government or law enforcement themselves must have been involved. Why could no suspects be found? Why was no evidence found to provide leads or draw conclusions? It was widely believed that a cover-up was conducted by one or both new suspects: law enforcement and the federal government. One at least must have been involved, with the possible complicity of the other.

The public could only remember two types of crimes this perfectly perpetrated. One involved priceless stolen works of art, not stolen politicians. The second was the failure to identify the leaker of the Supreme Court deliberations. In that supreme court investigation, there were only a handful of possible suspects compared to the governor's case, where at least half the population of the country, or more, could be considered suspects.

In the months that passed after the release of the governor, the newsworthiness of the ill-fated investigation had faded from the headlines. The governor, now freer to speak about his experience, began sharing his story with the media. As part of his public speeches, he discussed the events of his "time away," as he called it.

What was surprising to many was that, after going through such an ordeal, he did not seem angry or traumatized about his experience. In a change from his normally aggressive and combative style, he appeared almost stoic in his telling of his time in captivity. Some thought he might have read one of Nelson Mandela's or Senator John McCain's books about their time in captivity, whose time locked away was, of course, much lengthier, and more traumatic than that which the governor had experienced. Some thought the therapy that he surely must be participating in was having a quite remarkable effect. Whatever the reason behind the change, he was a different man now than before his time away.

He would joke about learning that he was called "the emperor" while being lectured by someone who, ironically, called themselves "his emperor." He would tell his audiences, "I cannot say that I agreed with the tactics, but the lessons were useful—extremely unwelcome, but useful, nonetheless." He talked about his experience of feeling powerless, feeling the anxiety of wondering how he was going to survive day-to-day at the mercy of someone who did not care one bit about what happened to him.

He still talked with passion about his agenda of saving the planet and helping those who needed help the most. The governor was more reasoned and more nuanced about plans and measurable progress. More importantly, he talked of the need to be more inclusive. Not in the new normal sense of color, race, gender, ethnicity, and all the other emerging diversities, but as citizens embracing "viewpoint diversity." He saw the state's citizens as one people, but with different opinions, sharing the same space, under leadership that listened to all those viewpoints within the boundary of what he called "this great state of ours."

He spoke of the various task forces and committees that he had working on the issues that were important to him and the citizens of his state. He had populated the committees with as wide a cross section of viewpoints as possible. He openly shared information and outcomes on a regular basis so that people could see what was being worked on. He invited input. He shared successes, setbacks, and elements of any impasse that needed to be resolved.

He told those in his audiences how much he had learned, not only from his own experience but from the many people he had met in the last several months. As he told them his story, they told him theirs. His conclusion at the end of his speeches was usually well received by his audiences. "In this country, in this state—what I had been doing is not how it should be! In my zeal to do my best, as I saw what was the best to do, I was creating as many problems or more, than I was solving. While my intent was always good, the outcome often fell short. It is time for all of us, as I have been doing, to step back and look at what we have spent, what it has purchased, for what result, and ask ourselves at what collateral costs? Above all, we must ask, how do we go forward TOGETHER? It is my job as governor of this state to provide leadership to all my constituents, providing leadership, and yes, even empathy, to all. It is my job to provide the framework, the opportunity, and the processes. It is my job to tap into the resourcefulness of ALL of those who wish to participate in the future development of this great state. To make it an example for the rest of the country about doing the hard work TOGETHER! Prospering TOGETHER! Making a shared, united, and better future TOGETHER!"

He had also realized that he could not solve climate change by himself or solely on the backs of his state's citizens. Yes, he argued, that as states and as a country, we needed to keep moving forward on improving the environment, but with a better transitional plan, one that would not make the US's own citizens pay for the sins of other polluters. The biggest contributor to carbon emissions had negotiated for longer timeframes to address their issues. They negotiated a slower, more reasoned transitional approach and were granted their demand.

The governor finally embraced the logic that if the country producing more carbon emissions than the rest of the world combined could take longer to address its problems, the US, with less than half of that environmental impact, should also be able to take a more realistic approach to addressing its issues. He accepted that he had been driving his state like it was the sole source of the world's climate problems when, in reality, his state was ranked among the lowest in contribution to emissions in the entire United States.

He was also aware that other countries were actively influencing and financing radical environmental groups in this country to eliminate our energy sources before the country was ready. He argued that these other countries were waging an ideological and financial war with us by using our own desires to be good global citizens against us.

Yes, he agreed that reducing and eventually eliminating fossil fuel-generated power plants would be a good thing. However, the subject of their continued existence continued to be debated for several reasons. One was that the replacement for existing capacity was not online yet and that we were not yet capable of being able to fulfill that need solely by renewable sources. Another was the technological improvements that the plants had made in reducing and scrubbing their emissions of environmental and other harmful content.

He stated that, for those reasons, until that capacity gap was filled, it was unwise to end an entire industry that was, at least for now, instrumental in meeting the state and national electrical requirements. It was argued that the existing plants had a role in meeting the substantially and continually increasing current and projected energy requirements of the state and the nation.

These facilities also had a necessary role in acting as a backup to the alternate forms of energy until those sources were proven fully capable of meeting the country's energy needs and those new sources were reliable for the long term. The reality remained, he had stated, that if the anticipated electrical capacity gap was not filled with sufficient and reliable alternatives to those plants, there would be major and potentially catastrophic issues to deal with in the event of their closure. In defense of his position, he could point to a state where a fossil fueled generation plant was brought online only during times when consumption exceeded or was expected to exceed the capacity of renewable source generation. Once the issue passed, the plant was idled until needed again. "Why lose that option?" he stressed.

He made it clear that once the transitions occurred and were proven successful, then yes, it would be time to let go of the old technology and embrace our renewable energy sources. He would support it wholeheartedly. Our citizens' well-being and the nation's security depended on getting it right!

While generally accepted as common sense, his reasoned arguments and pleas were met with resistance. The environmentalists called him a traitor. Some politicians ignored his logic. Others made speeches arguing against any retreat from our publicly stated and globally accepted commitments while those same politicians heaped praise upon our adversary for all that country's progress that paled in comparison. Only a few addressed the disparity between the US commitments as compared to the commitments of other countries and their longer timetables. There were too many legislators, lobbyists, and businesses that were making too much money themselves off those countries to provoke them. The president himself was often criticized as being owned, or at least significantly compromised, in that regard.

A group formed in the governor's state started an information and influence campaign against the greatest foreign contributors to global warming. It advocated that the citizens of his state stop buying products from those polluting countries. Not everyone agreed, but many did just that. The environmental protests in his state did not stop. What did happen was that people living in the relatively "safe to protest" culture of his state started to turn the spotlight on those offending country's policies and actions as well.

In his speeches, the governor discussed how his state had ranked among the top in crimes against its citizens. The work of his committees had yielded results. He had worked to have laws re-instituted that had worked previously but been discarded. Based on the work of his committees, new ways of addressing the problems of poverty, crime, and homelessness were implemented. Significant and measurable progress was being made at less cost.

When he felt that his voice was not being heard by the counties, the cities, the prosecutors, and the legislature to address the drugs and crime problems or the justice system reforms, he went straight to the people via speeches and media. He used the political capital he had acquired from his efforts for all the citizens to send the message that if the elected and appointed officials for their areas were not addressing their problems, it was incumbent upon them, the citizens, to replace them.

The choices belonged to them. "Decisions are affected by making your voice heard. Do not be silent and let the vocals ones direct your life," he would tell them. "Elections are won by those who show up and vote. Do not relinquish that precious individual right and privilege to organized groups who don't consider your interest along with the interest of those for whom they advocate." He advocated for voter integrity and election security, and pushed legislation to support it.

Even aside from his modified and more realistic environmental positions, as can be easily imagined, not everyone appreciated this different governor. Based upon the findings of the new committees, the poverty reduction plan had been revisited and adjustments made, recognizing new realities. Many of those who supported the old poverty reduction model and those who made significant sums of money from the "misery and victimization" movements, organizations, and businesses did not welcome this changed person who had always reacted positively to their requests and demands. Some advocacy groups who were losing control of their messages they had provided voters in the past challenged his data, findings, messages, and actions.

The radical left and others working for the destruction of what President Lincoln had called "this grand experiment" called him a traitor. They often disrupted his speaking engagements and protested his presence everywhere he went. Many of his staff resigned and actively worked against him. He had found it necessary to replace key members of his cabinet who refused to consider other points of view and possible solutions. Several in-state and out-of-state donors abandoned him and redirected their significant amounts of political money to those who would fight against him, all to further their own individual and collective agendas.

He simply replaced the workers who resigned with a mix of people with more divergent views. He praised the various opinions, more two-way discussions, better plans, and better decisions that accompanied a new mix of workers. The loss of the big money from out-of-state donors hurt, but he stood strong and defiant. His state stood by him and supported him for re-election.

He had changed, only in small part, because of what had happened to him during his time away. It was the real-life stories that he had heard. It involved including more view-diverse people in determining the causes of problems and possible solutions. The freshly reconstituted committees and task forces studied their given problems and the existing processes to address issues. Their analysis was used to determine opportunities for thoughtful, fully debated, and agreed-upon improvements.

It was realizing that not everything needed to be done at once. Priorities needed to be established, priorities that most of the population could agree on. This allowed costs to be spread over a longer time frame.

It was seeking other ways to accomplish solutions than the traditional knee-jerk reaction of simply throwing more tax money at the problems to show earnestness. It was conducting cost/benefit analyses that were published, debated in the legislature, released to the press, and posted on government websites.

It was creating clearly stated objectives to address individual issues that defined how performance to plan, progress, and costs would be measured and communicated on an ongoing basis.

It was recognizing that governing is a system. Understanding that pushing on one element of a problem in the system potentially creates another problem at another place in the system and breaking down and addressing those degrading linkages before implementation is crucial to success.

It was finding ways to reduce costs within the government programs before raising taxes.

It was the dismantling of the myriads of punishing fees, fines, and other financial punishments heaped upon the poor and middle class for simply being poor or for being unable to fight back against disparate treatment inherent in the system directed only toward them.

Above all, it was his leadership, using his pulpit, the power of the voice of his office, in creating disciplined, open processes and successful outcomes that made the real difference in the success that he experienced on several, but not all, fronts, over the next eight years. He was satisfied with what he had accomplished. Yes, it took longer than he wanted and required much more work than he had anticipated. But the engagement and involvement of the many had made so many more things, impossible before, successful now.

His state was united in a way that it had not been before. He believed that he had set his state on a steady course to deal with an uncertain future. He had worked hard and decided it was time for his own change. He chose not to stand for re-election. In a surprise move, he also chose not to endorse a successor. He felt that was a decision the state's citizens should make on their own, based on the candidates' positions on the issues that affected them.

He accepted a position at a major university that recruited him to teach courses in governance and leadership. He had received several lucrative offers; he chose the one that accepted his conditions regarding how he would teach his classes. He would teach the lessons that he had learned through his life the way he saw fit, not filtered through the ideological lens or legacy of the university. He decided to call his first course at the university "The Emperor's Lessons."

Made in the USA
Columbia, SC
29 December 2024

50826154R00081